AND THE WORLD WENT SILENT

Jacqueline Druga

Copyright © 2024 Jacqueline Druga

All rights reserved

The characters and events portrayed in this book are fictitious. Any similarity to real persons, living or dead, is coincidental and not intended by the author.

No part of this book may be reproduced, or stored in a retrieval system, or transmitted in any form or by any means, electronic, mechanical, photocopying, recording, or otherwise, without express written permission of the publisher.

Cover design by: Christian Bentulan

Special thanks to Paula for going out of her way to help me with this one.

CHAPTER ONE – MOTHER ABIGAIL

Is anybody out there?

I hadn't given up hope. Some would call what I did self-Isolation, but how could it be isolation when most of the world was gone? Some disappeared in the blink of an eye. Some went down fighting, but the end result was all the same. Very few of us remained.

There was a moment, a brief moment where I held out hope a lot more people had beaten the event. But what would be considered beaten?

I was alone. But not always. For the most part I was. I prefer it that way. It had been nearly 2 years since the event, and 21 months since I began the job. A job I took upon myself that eventually became official. It was an easy job. One that I hoped would keep me busy, but I knew better. I was in a small farmhouse, off a dirt road, 1.6 miles from the dead zone. From sunup to sundown, I sat in a rocking chair on the wooden front porch, like some old woman from a Stephen King novel, watching the dirt road or the cornfield waiting for someone to emerge.

Waiting.

Watching.

Since I got there, no one ever did. An animal, perhaps, one not normal. Sickly and dangerous. I would have to put it down and put it out of its pain, its misery. I hated that. But no survivors came.

I was ready for them, I waited for them, signs were placed everywhere, directing them down to the farm, for food, shelter and medical attention.

It was crazy that just 2 miles from where I sat, was toxic. A brief visit into the dead zone was safe. But it had to be brief. Yet the air I breathed from my home was fine. I checked daily.

Once in a while I would take the truck, start my timer and head into the dead zone. I never found anyone.

One hundred and eighty million people lived in the zone before the event, someone had to be alive.

Perhaps hiding for safety.

If they came out, I was one of several places in a nearly sixteen-hundred-mile radius spreading north to south they could find.

Not many safe houses.

Not many alive to receive them.

How I came to be at the house, living in solitude, waiting and watching for survivors wasn't out of an act of a need to serve humanity.

I ended up there out of selfishness.

It was the perfect location.

I wasn't watching the horizon of the dead zone waiting on just anyone to come through.

I was waiting and hoping they would come though.

The people I loved.

I wasn't giving up.

For them, I'd wait forever or die doing so.

CHAPTER TWO – THE BEFORE

BEFORE THE EVENT

"We will begin pre-boarding for flight 1515 for passengers who need assistance and families with small children."

I lifted my head when I heard the announcement. I didn't see any small children, but I did see a few people lined up in wheelchairs at the gate.

Not that the gate was crowded and not that I was a guru in air travel but judging by how many people there were in the seated area my flight didn't look too packed.

I was slightly nervous and excited. My first trip to Las Vegas. And even though it was labeled an educational convention, I planned on making the best of it.

It was my first solo trip anywhere. I had never gone away by myself. It felt nice, scary and exciting all at the same time.

Once every three years Mister Fudd's Furniture holds a convention in sin city and as team lead in our store, typically I wouldn't get a chance to go. But since our manager's wife was expecting and due any day, I was given the opportunity to take his place, and I didn't hesitate to accept.

At first, I thought I had to room with Belinda the manager from the Fairfield location. She seemed sort of fun and even started texting me about things we'd do. I had met her face to face only once, and when I didn't see her at the airport gate, I sent her a text. She said she also had a family emergency.

Perhaps later she'd come, but she didn't think so.

Wait.

My own hotel room.

It was getting even better.

My husband, however, was not thrilled about it. In the beginning, after I told him, I thought it was because I charged an upgrade to my seat, but it was about me leaving.

What the hell?

It wasn't like I went anywhere.

He made no bones about the fact he wasn't happy about me leaving. He used the excuse he was stuck caring for our two kids while I went off having fun.

Our kids were teenagers and old enough to fend for themselves.

I didn't quite understand it. As a pharmaceutical salesman, he went to more conventions than anyone I had ever met. Including Las Vegas. He had gone there two times the previous year. But me? I never went anywhere. I stayed home, always. I worked my job at a discount furniture store. I looked forward to the seminars. They sounded fun. How to make a better bed. How to teach people to take better care of cheap furniture. Even though we weren't allowed to say it was cheaper. They were affordable and less high quality.

Unlike my husband, I wasn't the salesman or a people person. I worked with helping people get approved on furniture loans. Much like the finance department at a car dealership.

His attitude was baffling. Getting angry any time I mentioned it the entire eight weeks before the trip. It wasn't as if I was never coming home, gambling away all of our money, or even having an affair. I didn't care about the motto 'what happens in Vegas stays in Vegas' I was just happy to go away, and the bonus was using the bathroom in peace with no one knocking on the door asking how much longer I'd be.

After a half dozen texts, I checked the battery life on my phone. It was still almost fully charged and I sent my husband a text telling him I was boarding and I had Wi-Fi on the plane and to tell the kids I would message them.

That was the last I spoke to my husband while I was at the airport. I probably would have texted more, but my attention was caught by a man arguing with a younger version of himself, who was probably his grown son.

"You didn't need to come," said the man. "No one is making you go to Gram's funeral. No one wants to see you pout."

"I'm not pouting. I'm also not saying I didn't want to come," the younger man replied. "I'm just saying you board in group one and I am boarding in group four."

"You bought a cheap seat?"

"I did. But you could have bought a better one for me."

"I could have," said the older man. "I didn't because you assumed."

"Fine. Whatever. Go enjoy the big seat."

"I will."

"I'll sit in the back alone."

"You do that."

The exchange made me inwardly laugh, I could see my own son doing this with his father. I looked forward to the day when my fourteen-year-old challenged my husband. Of course, I didn't know about the man near me, but I was willing to bet he was less of a prick than my husband.

Then again, maybe not.

They called our boarding group and I found myself standing right before the man who argued with his son. When we sat down, I was next to him.

We were in the first row, the 'big seats'. It wasn't first class by any means, just big seats with no one between you and one free adult beverage.

He placed my small bag in the overhead bin for me, which was nice.

Not saying anything, he gave a pleasant smile and nod as he sat down and stared forward watching the others board the plane. Almost as if he was waiting to see if his son came on.

He had to be in his late forties, maybe even fifty. The lines by his eyes and gray temples gave him a distinguished look.

With eyes forward he pretended to not pay attention when his son stepped on the plane.

I saw that.

The young man greeted the flight attendant and stopped at our row.

"Dad. I forgot my headphones."

The larger man behind him huffed and shook his head.

"You're holding up the line," said my seatmate.

"I forgot my headphones."

"Can you move?" asked the man behind him.

"Go around me," replied the young man.

"Do I look like I can go around you?"

The young man stepped into our row, it was tight and he bent down not to hit his head. His lanky frame was squished in there against his father's legs.

"Will, what the hell are you doing?" his father asked.

"Moving out of the way."

The flight attendant approached. "Sir, can you take your seat?"

"In a second, please," answered Will. "Dad, can I borrow yours?"

"No. I am using them."

"No, you won't. You'll drink and fall asleep."

"Who cares. They're mine and I had them in my ears already, why would you want something that's been in my ears?"

"I don't care, you're my dad."

"Go to your seat."

"Hold on," I spoke up and pulled my purse from my side to my lap. "I have an extra pair."

"For real?" Will asked.

"Yeah."

The father looked at me. "Don't give him your earbuds."

"They were a two pack and they're charged." I opened the case and handed him the earbuds. "Bluetooth and they're the airplane ones. They'll stop your ears from popping on takeoff."

"Thanks!" Will replied in an upbeat manner.

"You do know," the father pointed at the earbuds. "If you paid extra for that airplane popping preventative, you got ripped off. All earbuds will do that."

I shook my head and lied. "No, I didn't pay extra."

"Ignore him," said Will. "Once we're in the air, he'll down his free airplane bottle and be out like a light."

"Go to your seat."

"Thanks again. I'll give them back."

The father huffed. "You think she wants them back after they've been in your body?"

"I'm leaving."

"Thank God."

Waiting a few seconds, Will found his opportunity to exit our row.

"Kids," the man said. "You have any?"

"Two," I replied. "Fourteen and sixteen. Boy and girl."

"He's my only one." He then extended his hand. "Trace. Trace Miller."

I briefly shook his hand. "Shelby Arnold. Nice to know you."

"At least for four hours."

My phone beeped and I glanced down seeing it was another text from my husband, probably a nasty gram, and without opening it, I put my phone on airplane mode.

"You don't need to do that yet," Trace said.

"More than you realize I do." I placed my phone in my purse. "Now, how soon do we get to have those mini drinks?"

"Not soon enough."

CHAPTER THREE – THE BUILD UP

There wasn't much conversation between me and my seatmate Trace. After the initial, "Have you been to Vegas before?", we were in the air and fifteen minutes later, sipping on those baby bottles of booze.

He got out of me that I was in the furniture business, but I never found out what he did because his son was partially right.

Not long after Trace downed his drink, he put in those earbuds his son wanted, then closed his eyes.

I put in my earbuds and started streaming an episode of a British drama.

Two hours into our four-hour flight, through the corner of my eye, I noticed Trace trying to flag down a flight attendant. I actually worried for a moment the plane was going to crash, the way they were rushing up and down the aisles, whispering with each other and going in and out of the flight deck.

I removed an ear bud when the tone of a social media message broke through my show's dialogue. It annoyed me because it said Roy, my husband.

"Excuse me, Miss, I'm sorry, can I get another," Trace tried for her attention.

The flight attendant looked at him as if to say, 'how dare you', then took a few steps to the gallery, pulled out one of those narrow carts, and grabbed a square basket containing those little bottles.

I would have thought she would get a cup, glass of ice or

mixer, instead on her way to the back of the plane, she dropped it in his lap and said, "Help yourself."

"Okay …." Trace sung out the word, trying to catch the bottles as they bounced out and on to his lap.

"You think something is going on?"

"Um, yeah, they don't just drop booze on you. Probably an unruly passenger somewhere. It isn't a medical emergency though, they would have called for a doctor."

"Maybe we're going to crash."

"No. Do you know what the odds of that are?"

"Yes."

"What?" he asked.

"One in eight hundred and sixteen million, five hundred and forty-five thousand, nine hundred and twenty-nine. Or point zero, zero, zero twelve percent. Something like that."

"Something like that."

"I looked it up."

"I'm sure." Trace grabbed a tiny bottle from the basket and uncapped it. He showed me the basket. "Have some."

"Maybe in a bit. That's a lot of booze."

"Eh, I'm a professional, this is nothing."

I didn't know what he meant by that until he downed that entire bottle.

Did he notice my wide eyes as he did so?

He recapped the bottle and placed the empty one in the pouch on the wall in front of us. Then leaning forward, he turned his body and looked down the aisle.

"See anything?"

"They're standing there talking." He stood. "Unruly passenger. Excuse me." He walked to the bathroom in front.

My phone vibrated from another message and I opened it.

'Get home,' the message from Roy read.

I replied, mumming my response as I typed. "I am in the air asshole."

Bling.

"When you land get the next flight back."

"Oh, I am not doing this today." Shaking my head, I made sure I had my earbuds and I made my way out of the seat.

It was always my plan to video message the kids on social media using the Wi-Fi, it wasn't my plan to fight with my husband.

He needed to stop and calm down.

The kids didn't need to see him getting angry over something so trivial.

Realizing Trace was in the front bathroom, I headed to the back of the plane. At the very least I could find out what was going on.

All four flight attendants were at the back of the plane. Three in the aisle while one male attendant was standing before a bathroom door.

He knocked on the door. "Sir, I know you said you're fine. But you have been in there a while. You need to come out. Don't make me call the captain." He looked toward another attendant and whispered. "Go get the captain."

It felt a little awkward stepping into the drama and making my way into the bathroom across from them. But they didn't stop me, so it couldn't have been that bad. I was relieved it was someone taking too long in the bathroom rather than a medical emergency or pending crash.

However, there was a chance that I would be the next person they were rushing out of the toilet.

I stepped in, latched the door and placed in my earbuds.

Although it wasn't a phone call and over the internet, I was still worried I was going to interfere somehow with the flight controls.

Make it brief, I told myself.

Be stern.

My friends always told me he was controlling, but after twenty years, I knew how to handle him.

I opened the social media messenger app and hit 'video chat' next to Roy's name.

It didn't take long for him to answer.

"Shelb, get home."

The connection wasn't great, a combination of being in the air and the bathroom.

"Get home," he repeated.

In a low, angry whisper I growled at him. "Are you kidding me? I'm on a freaking plane. What am I supposed to do, jump out?"

"No, listen to me …"

"Roy. No."

"Mom?" my son appeared in the background.

"Oh, hey Alex sweetie. I have to go, I'm hiding in the bathroom. Calm your father down please."

"Shelb!" Roy snapped.

"Oh, no, you are not yelling at me."

My daughter Layla stepped into the camera shot. "Mom, Dad is …"

"I know he's out of control. Calm him down. Love you guys," I said pleasantly. "I have to go before they start pounding on the door."

"Shelb, when you land you get on the next flight back."

"Roy. We'll discuss this later."

"Shelb, you aren't—"

After a quick rush of static, the video call screen turned completely white. The controls, like the stop and other effects were still showing, but it was nothing but white on the screen. Before I could even register that, high pitch feedback rang out. It didn't sound like it was coming from my earbuds, but it couldn't be from anything else.

Just as I reached to wipe them from my ears, the plane dipped and tilted violently. I was lifted at least a foot in the air, hitting my head on the bathroom ceiling. Not hard, but hard enough I felt it. When the plane normalized, I came back down. My knee hit against the commode and my phone dropped to the floor.

What happened?

Did I cause it by using my phone? The plane seemed steady now.

Hand shaking, more scared than anything, I reached down for my phone.

I cringed a little not just from the ache in my knee, but the thought of what my phone touched.

Hurriedly, I washed my hands, then using a wet towel, wiped off my phone.

It was time to get out of there. At least I didn't have to worry about them scolding me for taking too long. More than likely, they were dealing with passengers after the dip and tilt that happened.

Unlatching the door, I readied to step out.

Little did I know, I wouldn't be ready for what I would face.

CHAPTER FOUR – LOCKED IN

Why wouldn't the door open? Was someone keeping me in? Holding the door closed? I couldn't hear anything, then again, the engine noise made it impossible.

I took a moment, then tried again.

Nothing.

In my attempts to get the door open, the adrenaline rush from the plummeting then recovering plane, started to ease and was quickly replaced with fear.

Something had happened.

Was I in some sort of trouble for using my phone in a communication manner even though it wasn't through Wi-Fi? Was it just a coincidence the plane dropped while I was talking to Roy?

Roy. Immediately I went back to my phone, opened the app and tried again to video call him.

It rang and rang and no one answered.

Again, I tried the door.

I shoved it, I double checked the lock. I was stuck. Maybe I wasn't in trouble. Maybe something happened to the door when the incident occurred.

Hating to do it, I started knocking on the door.

"Anyone? Can anyone hear me? I'm stuck in here. Hello?"

I waited another minute and tried again, this time harder with the knocking and louder with my voice.

"Can anyone hear me? Help! I'm locked in the bathroom. Someone!"

My hand started hurting from banging, I switched fists. It wasn't as loud with my left hand.

Take a break I told myself, and when I stepped back for a moment, my hand on the sink's edge, I heard the click.

The door opened and Trace stood there.

The thought that I must have looked really dumb lasted only a second when I saw his face. He didn't look as confident nor as calm as he did when he got up to go to the bathroom.

"Thank you," I gushed out. "I thought I'd be stuck here the whole time." I moved to leave, but he blocked the doorway.

"Shelby, listen, something ... something has happened." He looked over his shoulder then back to me.

"You mean when the plane dropped."

"More than that. I just need you to be prepared."

"For what?"

"It's bad."

"What happened? What?" I asked with urgency and concern.

Trace stepped back, giving me space to get out.

I wasn't even through the narrow doorway of the bathroom when I saw the legs on the floor. The blue slacks told me it was the male flight attendant that was knocking on the other bathroom door.

It wasn't what I expected to see, not even close. It caused me to lose my breath for a moment and step back into the bathroom.

"It's just the beginning," Trace said. "You can't stay in there you have to come out."

"What's just the beginning?"

He choked on his words. "It's everyone. Not just the flight attendant. Everyone is dead."

CHAPTER FIVE – FLOATING

Fear of heights, being nervous, fear of rejection. Haunted houses, airplanes, fear of the truth. All of them were every day negative scares a human being faced.

Anything that scared me or caused me fear before the moment I stepped out of the bathroom paled in comparison to what I saw.

Sheer terror swept over me. There were so many compartments they all joined together to make one major ball of terror.

I was so overly terrified my body trembled, my heart raced and voice cracked. Yet, I felt mentally calm and rational.

I should have screamed, perhaps I was in shock. That had to be it.

I walked cautiously trying to decipher what I was seeing.

A female flight attendant lay across a seat on top of the passengers.

Arms of people dangled down as they slumped toward the aisle. Some fell forward.

Trace, a stranger, held my hand leading me up the aisle. "I can't look at them. I can't."

Then I had to.

"Did you see what happened?" I asked.

"I was in the bathroom. Just as I went to open the door, the plane jolted and I was thrown. I'm a big man to be thrown in such a small space."

I was thrown, too, I hit the ceiling."

"You're lucky you didn't break your neck."

I wanted to respond with 'like some of the passengers' because it was evident that's what happened.

A woman in 47E had her face pressed against the seat in front of her, and her head was nearly turned all the way around like an exorcist movie.

A few rows up, a man sitting in an aisle seat of row 39 made me stop. His body extended outward into the aisle, his arm touching the floor. His neck was arched drastically bringing his head back.

His mouth was open, but it was his eyes that caught my attention.

The whites of his eyes were still white, but the color part was a silverish blue, like a color contact lens.

That was when I saw the blood. A small amount, almost minuscule, came from his ear. Because of the way his head was positioned, it flowed to the temple.

I pivoted quickly to the row across from them and looked at the three people there. They were overlapping. The window seat and aisle seat passenger fell on the middle seat and he slumped over them.

I was going to keep walking until I saw the blood on the middle seat man's ear. Not a lot, but just like the man behind him.

Reaching in, hating to do it, I grabbed the man in the middle and moved him until his head turned.

It was a slight jump scare the way he just plopped. He was still warm, so I felt for a pulse.

"What are you doing?" asked Trace.

"He's still warm."

"He just died. Everyone just died."

"How? And his eyes," I said. "They're weird."

"What do you mean weird?"

"Like he's wearing a silver blue contact."

"Corneal opacity, it's what happens when a person dies."

"This fast? And the blood?"

Finally, Trace turned and looked. "It doesn't look like trauma. I don't know why the eyes look like this." He took a step back and checked on the person in the next row. "All their eyes are like this."

"Could there have been a chemical attack on the plane? Something with pressure? Something we missed because we were in the bathroom?"

"It could be. I mean everyone was hit all at … shit."

"What?"

Trace spun and hurriedly raced up the aisle. "The pilot."

That thought hadn't even crossed my mind. If the same happened to the pilot and copilot, then we were doomed, not because we couldn't fly the plane, but the flight deck door would be locked and we wouldn't even be able to try.

I made it to the front of the plane shortly after Trace. He stood in that galley part.

The flight deck door was open and a body lay there, it was the captain or copilot, in the doorway keeping it from locking.

He either died walking out or died trying to keep it open.

Trace stepped over the body and looked into the cockpit. After a second, he looked at me and shook his head.

I sighed out, arms folded against my body and turned. When I did, my eyes caught the empty seat in the back and my stomach sunk.

"Trace. Where was your son seated?"

"In the back. I couldn't look."

"There's an empty seat. I wonder if he was the person in the bathroom they couldn't get out."

Before I could say anymore, Trace rushed by me returning to the back of the plane.

"Will!" Trace pounded on the door. "Will are you in there!"

When I passed the row with an empty seat, I made sure I didn't see the young man on the floor. He wasn't.

How painful and torturous it had to be for Trace, his son was on board the doomed flight.

He had to hold on to hope that Will, like Trace and I, was fine because for some reason the bathroom protected him.

"Will!" Trace kept pounding. "Open up. Will are you in there?"

"Can you kick it down?" I asked. "It opens inward."

"Good idea." Will stepped back and gave a heaving kick to the door.

It didn't budge.

He tried it again.

I understood what he was feeling. It was his child, no matter how old or young, it was his kid and he needed to get to him.

Again, his foot slammed against the door.

"Want me to try?" I asked.

Trace looked at me.

"Maybe I can loosen it."

After nodding, Trace held out his hand. "Be my guest."

Click-click.

We both looked at the door when it unlatched.

It opened and slowly, Will, his face covered in blood, staggered out.

CHAPTER SIX – THE WOMAN IN SIX C

Will's reaction to what he saw was not what I expected from a young man who seemed carefree and chill. It could have been a head injury, because of a cut on the top of his head near the hairline.

Basically, he freaked out. Like some scared kid walking through a fright house on Halloween.

Looking left to right at every person, shaking his head, muttering "no" over and over.

Finally, we brought him to our front row. The people in the two seats across from us were still visible, but they looked more like they were sleeping when I closed their eyes.

I found a first aid kit in the kitchen and using a cleaning towel and bottled water, I wiped his face and sought the origin of the bleeding.

I touched the gash on his head. "I don't think you need stitches," I said. "The head just bleeds a lot."

"Are you a nurse or doctor?" asked Will.

"No, just a mom. I finance furniture at Mr. Fudd's."

I shook the cold pack to activate it. "Once this feels cold put this on your head."

"What do you think Dad?" Will asked.

"I think whatever she says sounds good."

"Let's of bleeding heads with my son," I told him and went to sit in the other seat. The small basket of booze was there. "Think I might have one now." I took a bottle of vodka and before placing the basket on the floor I offered one to Will. "Want one?"

Before Will could answer, Trace did. "No. He doesn't."

Will glanced at his father than to me. "No thank you. What happened? Do we know?"

"No. Something hit everyone instantly. Like a gas leak," I said. "Or maybe a terror attack."

Trace asked. "Will, what were you doing in the bathroom?"

"Going to the bathroom."

"No, really, what were you doing?" Trace repeated. "Obviously, you were in there a while if they were trying to get you out."

"I know."

"What were you doing?"

"Dad …"

"Trace," I tried to intervene. "Maybe we try to talk about the situation at hand."

"Were you using?" Trace asked hard, ignoring me. "Is that why you wouldn't open up. You were using."

"Dad."

"Trace."

"Shelby, this isn't your business."

"No shit, it's not my business, but is now the time?"

"I don't need a stranger giving me advice." Trace looked at Will. 'They were trying to get you out."

"I wasn't using."

"Right."

"No, I wasn't using," Will snapped. "I was sick. I was stuck on the toilet and it didn't help with them pounding and pounding. Then whatever happened, happened. I woke up on the floor, bleeding with my pants around my ankles and a pounding at the door. So no, again, I wasn't using. I've been clean and sober for six months. At least I can make that claim."

"Are you okay?" I asked Will. "I know it's none of my business, but you're alive, if you were my kid, right now that is all that matters." I took a sip of my vodka, then looked at Will. "Shit. Sorry."

"Alcohol wasn't his thing," Trace said.

"Can we talk about the situation at hand," I asked.

"Yeah, dad, I think there are more pressing issues than my long bathroom stunt," Will said, "Like who's flying the plane and how the hell are we going to land?"

Nowhere in my wildest imagination did I think what happened on that plane was happening on a global scale. If I did, my mind would have been on my children.

To me, it was the plane. It was the focus we had to conquer. If I wanted to get home or even land alive, we had to go on the flight deck.

We also needed to get off the plane.

So many bodies.

Trace removed the pilot and the co-pilot's bodies, placing them in the other front row seat. I located a blanket in the flight attendant section and covered the seat as best as I could.

When I returned to the flight deck, I saw both father and son just staring at the controls.

"Uh, yeah," I said. "This isn't going to be easy. Maybe there's an instruction book."

"Why would they have an instruction book?" Trace asked.

"For a situation like this. I mean someone had to think about it. At least we're one step better than if the door was closed and locked."

Trace tossed out his hands. "Maybe we can radio someone. They can walk us through it."

"Or look it up," Will said. "Wi-Fi. We can go look up how to land a commercial jet."

"That's a good idea," I told him. "We can do that. Like a flight tutorial."

"My phone is smashed," said Will. "How about yours?"

"It's on the seat."

"That means you have to go into the main cabin." Will looked back. "I still see all the bodies."

Trace replied. "You're going to, everyone on the plane but us is dead."

"You don't think they're gonna …." Will grunted. "Get up, do you?"

I asked. "You mean like maybe they're sleeping?"

"No, like maybe they're dead," Will said. "And they're gonna get up and attack."

"Like zombies?"

"Yeah." Will nodded. "It already feels like something in a movie."

"About that time," I said. "If that happens, we lock this door."

"But would it be morally responsible landing a plane full of the undead?"

Trace exhaled heavily, probably more of a huff. "What the hell is the matter with you? They aren't going to turn into zombies. They aren't going to attack. They're there, dead. No one is getting up."

At that second Will grunted a screaming, "Uh!" and pointed.

I hurriedly spun around to look and sure enough, I saw what scared him.

A man stood in the aisle near the back of the plane, he looked around. He was a younger man from what I could see, he wore a short sleeve white shirt and dress pants.

"We need a weapon," Will whispered.

The man turned and faced us.

"Shit," said Will. "Shut the door."

"I don't think he's a zombie," I said.

"He is."

The man rushed forward to us.

"Shut the door. Shut the door. Shut the door," Will panicked.

"Will you knock it off." Trace stood.

The man arrived in the hallway before the flight deck. He had one of those dark sleeping masks on his head as if he lifted it from his eyes and perched them on his hair, like people do with sunglasses.

"Where's the pilot?" he asked.

Nervously I pointed backward. I would be lying if I didn't say I was scared, and for a split second I wondered if Will was right.

He shook his head and walked onto the flight deck, immediately sitting in the left seat.

He didn't hesitate. He checked out the controls, adjusted something, then lifted the radio.

"This is flight one, five, one five Big Blue. We have a situation. Anyone copy, over?"

He repeated it again.

Nothing.

Obviously, he then switched channels. "Ground, this is one five, one five, can anyone hear me? Is anyone there? Over."

He gave it a minute.

"Anyone there?"

"Why isn't anyone answering?" I asked.

He shrugged and set down the radio. "Could be something happened to the plane. The controls look good though. However out there tells a different story." He turned some in the chair. "Does anyone know what happened?"

"Dude," Will said. "How are you alive? You weren't in the bathroom."

"What does that have to do with it?" he asked.

Will swirled his finger around. "We were all in the bathroom when it happened. Not the same one."

"Clearly. I was sleeping and I woke up."

Trace shook his head slightly. "You didn't feel the plane drop or tilt?"

"I'm a heavy sleeper, and I took something to sleep. I'm surprised I woke up. You guys thought I was dead?"

I replied. "Everyone else is."

"Are they?" he asked. "Did you check? Because I wasn't dead."

"We didn't check," Trace said. "We were worried about how we were going to land."

"I got this. I think you should check the others."

"What do you mean, you got this?" Trace asked.

Will added. "Are you going on the internet?"

"No, I'm a pilot. Or was," he replied. "My license is suspended for drinking on the job."

Will let out a single, "Ha' then stifled his laugh. "Sorry, just you and my dad might be good friends."

Irritated, Trace sighed out his son's name. "Will. Go check bodies."

"No."

"Go check the bodies!"

"What are you going to do?"

"I'm going to help this man out."

"Why don't I help this man …"

"Go."

I grabbed Will's arm. "I'll go with you."

"Fine. Start from the back?"

"Might as well."

It looked worse when I walked to the back of the plane with Will. My shock had worn off and reality started to set in.

I wanted to freak out, be hysterical, but there was no point to it. I couldn't run away from the plane of death. We were stuck there, and the only thing that would make it better is stepping off the plane.

The event that happened on the plane had to of caused the radio malfunction also. They probably were trying to reach us as much as we were trying to reach them.

I wanted to think it was easy to tell who was dead and who was not, but clearly the man with the sleeping mask proved that wrong.

The eyes and blood on the ears were a good sign of death, but the one person I touched was warm.

Maybe whatever chemical weapon was used affected everyone in a way and they were just passed out and not dead.

It didn't explain the sleeping mask guy.

I had to reassess my ability to know if I were feeling for a pulse or not.

The first body I touched in the back of the plane was cooler and not like the woman I checked earlier.

The body was that of a man, his eyes were that blue silver and a small amount of blood was on his ears. I was pretty confident he didn't have a pulse and I moved to the next person.

Cold.

Dead.

"She's dead," said Will across the aisle. "Him, too."

"Are you sure?"

"Yeah. Cold."

Then I thought of that woman I touched. Her eyes wide, blood in her ears, yet she was warm.

I turned thinking I would go find her when I heard this groan. This loud scared groan. Like someone was trying to cry and their tongue was cut out.

"That," Will said. "Is a zombie cry."

"It can't be." I looked and saw a woman standing.

She was near to the front of the plane. Her arms flailing about and she kept turning around in circles. Hands out, swinging, then feeling.

Crying out again, I swore it sounded like "Help" and I hurried her way.

"Shelby, what are you doing?" Will yelled. "This is how they get you."

"She's hurt."

"She's undead."

"Will. No. I'm telling you."

I arrived at row six, she was in the middle seat, seemingly trapped.

Her face wasn't pale, she still had color, but her eyes … her eyes were gone, the same color the dead bodies had.

"Ma'am," I called to her.

She didn't stop or even seem to notice I was there.

"Ma'am," I tried calling for her again.

"Shelby." Will rushed to me. "Come on. Leave her."

"Go get your father."

"Fine."

I reached for the woman to let her know I was there.

Maybe with her eyes like that she couldn't see me. The moment my hand touched her arm, she swung out wildly, crying and screaming.

She smacked my hand away and I tried again. Bringing my hands to her, gently touching her first, then again.

She calmed down.

I placed my hand on her wrist and immediately she felt for my arms with her other hand.

She couldn't see.

When she grabbed my hand, she gripped it. She was trembling, scared, she stopped screaming when she felt me. I knew she wasn't a threat. She was scared. I would be too. I knew the way she held my hand she was relieved that I somehow found her in this new darkness.

I didn't know what else to do with her. I would have to eventually get her out of that row. But what then? Could I help her?

Something horrible happened on our flight, and it wasn't just the death.

And if she was alive, I was willing to bet we missed others that were, too.

CHAPTER SEVEN – FIGURING IT OUT

I didn't even know his name. All I knew of him was that he was a pilot, was sleeping and still hadn't taken that sleep mask off the top of his head.

I was more concerned with the woman I named Mary. She sat in the big seat, she couldn't speak correctly. It was like her words were jumbled. Most uninterpretable. She held onto my hand for dear life.

I uncapped a little bottle of wine, brought it to her nose for her to smell, then cupped her hand around it.

With my help she brought it to her mouth and sipped.

"Here's the situation," Sleep mask man said as he stood by our front seat. "I can't reach anyone. We have an hour more to go until we reach Vegas. That's where we need to aim for. Maybe get some answers. But I think it's all the plane. Communication breakdown. Some sort of attack. Has anyone else gotten up?"

I shook my head. "Just Mary here. And I am pretty sure her blindness and whatever else is going on with her happened on the plane."

"We'll request medical assistance when we land. Hopefully by then we'll make radio contact. If not, I am sure they are looking for us."

"What is your name?" asked Trace. "You never said."

"Wren," he replied. "I'm sorry I didn't say. I'm not much of a talker and I'm going to head back to the flight deck. Keep me posted of anything else that happens back here."

I stayed there in the front, watching Wren as he walked back and left the door open.

"So, tell me about her," Trace said.

"I don't know, she just got up."

Will stood in the aisle, one arm folded over his waist while biting his nails. "I'm not going back there again."

"We were checking pulses and she stood. She's trying to talk," I continued, "It's hard to understand. I know she can't see and I don't think she can hear."

"So strange." Trace eyed the mini bottles and grabbed one.

"I know the blindness happened here," I added. "I watched everyone get on the plane. No one that I could tell was blind nor had eyes like hers. Maybe she was deaf beforehand."

"Uh-ah," replied Will. "Gram was deaf. Mary's arms waved about, had she been deaf she would have been signing."

"I agree," said Trace. "Blood on the ears, the eyes. What the hell happened on this plane?"

"I think it was an attack," I said. "I really do. Maybe a gas or weapon that hits the brain, but in some people, it didn't touch all the way or at all. The brain because that controls sight and hearing."

"Got to be a point of entry. Right?" Trace asked.

"What do you think Dad?" Will asked.

"Eyes. The eyes are a route of transmission." He took a step back and turned facing the cockpit. "Wren did you have your sleep mask on?"

"I did," Wren replied. "And my earbuds, I was out."

I drew up a thinking look and Trace must have noticed.

"What is it?" Trace asked. "What are you thinking?"

"Blood coming out of the ears. Not a lot," I replied. "I had my earbuds in."

"Me, too," said Will.

"Me, as well," added Trace.

"And we were in the bathroom," I said. "But it doesn't make sense. A chemical or gas wouldn't need your ears or eyes, it would go through the air. Then again, I'm no doctor or scientist."

"I am," Trace said.

"Which one?" I asked.

"Doctor. And you're right. It doesn't add up. I'm not gonna second guess this. Not until we land. We have about an hour. We'll get answers then and get Mary some help."

"Dad, what would cause her eyes to get like that?" Will asked.

"I don't know." Trace crouched down and looked at Mary. "I've never seen anything like this unless the person was dead."

"Uh!" Will shirked.

"She's not dead." Trace grabbed her wrist. "She's warm, she has a heartbeat and is breathing. She's scared. I would be, too."

"What if this is everywhere?" Will asked. "I mean, what if it happened everywhere and not just the plane?"

"Please, don't say that," I told him. "Please. I Lost connection with my husband when this happened."

Trace looked at me. "What do you mean?"

"I was doing the messenger video chat. And he dropped out at the same time the plane did that drop," I explained.

"What did you see?" Trace asked.

"Nothing. The screen washed out," I explained. "I heard feedback. Right before I flew up and hit my head."

Trace stood upright. "The brain is complex. But this is baffling. I think it is something that affects the brain. But the side of the brain controls hearing, the back is vision, so whatever it was, if indeed it hit the brain, it hits the whole brain killing them. Maybe it didn't hit Mary as hard as the others. Maybe she was sleeping. Who knows? She seems calm, scared, but calm, so her frontal lobe wasn't affected."

"What is that?"

"Emotions, reactions." Trace shook his head. "She's drinking wine so that part of her brain is fine. Taste, smell. Like I said. I'm not going to overthink this. Let those on the ground figure this out."

"Mary seems okay now." I laid my hand on her giving her a reassuring squeeze. "Still upset though."

"Wouldn't you be?" Will asked.

"Without a doubt." I stood up.

"Where are you going?" Will questioned.

"Well, seeing that our lives are now in the hand of a man who is still wearing he sleep mask on his head, I want to talk to him."

I walked to the cockpit and called out as I entered. "Hey."

"Hey," he replied.

I sat down in the seat to the right. "Do you need help?"

"Do you know how to fly?"

"No. But I thought I'd ask. I'm Shelby or Shelb or Shel whatever you want to call me."

"Nice to meet you. Wish it was under better circumstances."

"Do you really think there's something wrong with the radio?"

Wren hesitated before answering then nodded. "Yeah. What's happening back there."

"Nothing. Just Mary drinking wine, calming down. I found out Trace is a doctor."

"Well, that's good. What does he say?" Wren asked.

"Not much. He said he wants to wait until we land." I stared out. "This is a great view. I wish this attack wasn't the reason for it, I'd enjoy it more."

"Me, too."

"I have to tell you," I said. "It's a good thing you're a pilot. You came out of nowhere."

"Not really, the back of the plane," he said. "I woke up, stood, and saw everyone was, well, dead. Then I realized, who was flying the plane."

"Are you an airline pilot?" I asked. "For like a certain airline?"

"No and yes," he replied. "I flew for the Airforce my entire career. The last four years for Airforce one."

"No shit."

"No shit."

"What happened?" I asked. "I mean you don't have to tell me."

"I had a beer. One beer. I was in my hotel room," he replied. "I thought there was no way the president would need flown anywhere at eleven at night. So, like I said, I had a beer, but technically I was on duty and on call."

"He needed a flight."

Wren nodded. "Who would have thought that late. Never happens."

"So, the president called you out?" I asked.

"No, the other pilot turned me in. He said he smelled alcohol. He was right. I was removed immediately and placed on suspension."

"Wow, suspension. A part of me thinks you lucked out, it could have been worse."

"The president had my back."

"When was this?" I asked. "I'm sorry, I don't mean to act like a reporter."

"A week ago. I was on my way to Vegas to interview for a job and … here we are."

"I hope the interview goes well. Make sure you tell them you jumped to the pilot's seat."

"I'm thinking once we land, the news will have that covered."

"Shelb!" Will called my name. "Shelby."

"Excuse me." I stood up and walked from the flight deck. I didn't need to ask what he wanted, I saw.

At least eight people had stood up. They moved back and forth like Mary had, only these people sounded a little different. They weren't trying to form words, they were crying out, groaning, in a painful way.

"What do we do?" Will asked.

"They're confused and lost," said Trace. "Woke up to not being able to see, maybe not even hear. Let's move them up here."

"Dad, there's bodies up here. It was hard enough to get Mary to understand."

"Then we do one at a time." Trace suggested. "We have two seats up here. Let's start in the back. Start bringing them up."

Something about it was off to me. It felt different than Mary, they seemed different.

While they did move in circles, left to right, clearly unable to see, they didn't flail their arms. They all cried out the same way, heads back, necks arched.

"Trace, maybe we should let them go until we land," I said.

"They're sick, Shelb, we can't do that. We didn't let Mary go." He walked forward leading the way.

Most of those standing were in the middle of the plane. Not far apart from each other. As if the middle was somehow affected differently than the rest of the plane.

"Just gently reach out," Trace said. "Like you did with Mary. Give a reassuring hand, calming them."

When he said that I noticed all eight of them turned, they caught the sound of his voice.

"Trace," I said. "They hear you. They can hear."

"You think?" Trace asked.

"I'm out," said Will, backing up. "This is freaky."

"Stop," Trace ordered. "These people need our help."

"I don't care."

I looked back to see Will racing back up the aisle.

Trace called out. "Hello. I know you're scared. If you can hear me. We're going to help you as best as we can."

Then something odd happened. Something that sent shivers down my spine and all alerts in my brain went off.

All eight of them turned rigidly to the sound of Trace's voice. Locked in.

All of their eyes were that color gray, yet, they had focus by hearing his voice. There was something about that moment. Something frightening.

"Trace." I reached out to his shirt, grabbed on to the back. "Let's go."

"What is the matter with you?" Trace asked.

He didn't have to wait long for an answer on why I was concerned.

They followed the sound of our voices.

All eight of them leapt forward. Over seats, over other passengers and they moved with force I could only describe as enraged.

"Trace!" I screamed.

That was a mistake.

They tilted their heads, locking in on the sound and even without sight, they locked in on us.

The first of the eight arrived head of the pack. His arms swung out violently. It wasn't like Mary who reached out for answers and help, this man swung out in an attack.

He struck Trace. The hit sent Trace back some into me. And the man continued to swing over and over.

The others joined in, trying to get to Trace.

What was happening?

I grabbed Trace, pulling at him.

Whispering I said, "Quiet. They can't see."

I moved backwards with him at a fast pace and when there were a few aisles separating us from the eight, suddenly they were confused again. Looking around, groaning out.

We slowed down, taking quiet steps to the front of the plane.

When Trace turned, I noticed his face was bleeding, a gash on his cheek. I gave the 'shush' signal, finger to my mouth to Will before he could say anything.

I could tell by the look on Will's face he was confused.

Moving his mouth, Will did sign language to Trace. And Trace only shook his head, making his way to the bathroom.

I didn't feel safe back there. Eight of them were lingering in the aisle a few rows from where we were.

After pointing to the cockpit, I then pointed to Mary. Trying to convey quietly that we needed to go there.

Will nodded.

When I got his acknowledgement, I went to the bathroom. Trace was washing his face in the small sink.

In the lowest volume whisper I could possibly muster, I said. "They seem violent."

Trace nodded then pointed to his forehead.

"So, it hit there on them?"

"Shh."

In my mind there was no way they could hear us in the

bathroom, not with the engine noise.

But they could hear Mary.

I did.

Will must have been trying to move her and when he did, she cried out.

I backed up from the bathroom into that little area between the flight deck and galley.

All eight of them were rushing forward up the aisle.

At the front, by our row, Mary stood screaming, crying, like a beacon of light for them to follow in the darkness.

No amount of telling her to be quiet would help.

Will tried to pull her back, but she was freaking out.

Then Wren yelled out, "What's going on back there?"

Wrong thing to do.

The eight of them moved faster.

Maybe it was fear, or his young age, I don't know. But Will gave up on Mary.

He left her. I didn't understand why at the moment. How could he just leave her?

I felt him brush me as he stood near the flight deck door and I moved for Mary.

Just as my hand reached for her, two passengers pounced on her knocking her to the ground.

She still screamed in fear.

I wished she would stop, but she didn't.

One, two, three and then like a mound of ants on a crumb, they encompassed her in a heap.

Her screams muffled, going from fear to pain then silent.

There was nothing I could do. I wanted to help her. And I knew at that second, why Will abandoned her.

If he hadn't, Will, like her, would have been under that mound.

Our safety space was small. There was only one place to go.

I don't know who grabbed me, Will or Trace, but before I knew it, I was pulled back onto that flight deck and the door closed.

Utter confusion and fear went through me as I stared at the closed door.

Those on the other side were fueled by anger, moving on sound and acting with violence.

How was this even happening?

What was happening?

I placed my hand on the closed door, my eye shifted to the camera monitor.

They were fighting each other, battling.

We didn't have much time until we landed.

Until we were safe.

And hopefully get some answers to the madness we faced thirty thousand feet in the air.

CHAPTER EIGHT – THIRTY THOUSAND FEET UP

"Lock the door," I told Will.

"They can't open it," Will replied.

Wren interjected. "They can't, he's right. Only we can open that door once it's sealed."

"I was thinking of a different reason," Will said. "Anyhow …" He looked up at the small monitor just outside the door. "They're out there."

"So is our water," I commented, watching the screen as well. "Good thing we're close to landing. Because the bathroom is out there, too."

"Can someone tell me what's going on?" Wren asked. "And where is Mary?"

I watched Will suck in his bottom lip.

"It's not your fault," I told him.

"Why would it be my fault?"

"Because you backed up."

"So, you're saying it's my fault?" asked Will.

"No, I'm saying it's not your fault," I defended.

"But you said, it's not my fault that I backed up."

"I'm saying it's not your fault she's dead."

"What?" Wren blasted. "Mary is dead?"

"They killed her." I pointed to the screen. "Beat her, but I'm not sure if they knew what they were doing."

"How did she die?" Wren asked. "Other than being pulverized. She was deaf, blind, helpless."

Trace spoke up. "It was a survival choice. They were all coming fast, they were on Mary so fast and there was nothing we could do. I had to stop Shelb from trying to help."

"This is crazy," Wren said. "What the hell kind of chemical did they release?"

"Whatever it is," Trace said. "It affects people differently. Mary couldn't see or hear, these people can hear, but I don't think they can see."

"We might find someone out there," I said. "That can't hear but can see."

Trace shrugged.

"Do you think the others will wake up?" Wren asked.

Trace shook his head. "I don't know. I do know that when we land, we need help getting past them out there." He sat down. "They're drawn by sound. And it seems they're waiting by the last place they heard us."

Watching the screen, I looked at each of them. They seemed calm, not like they were moments earlier. "I wonder what made them stop beating Mary. I mean, did they know she was dead or was it the lack of sound."

"I have an idea," said Wren and he pressed a button. "Will those passengers standing by the cockpit door, please move to the back."

I kind of cringed in embarrassment for him. That wasn't going to work, they didn't understand things, they reacted to sound.

Just as I was about to mom-splain, I watched the eight of them run from the door to the back of the plane. "That worked."

"You said they follow sound. Now I have a recording playing back there," stated Wren.

But the eight of them vacating the area left me with a view of Mary. Her body was a twisted wrangled mess. I felt so bad for her. To be in the dark, to not hear and suddenly being hurt.

It had to have been horrifying for her.

I watched, saying a silent prayer for the woman I didn't know. It was a terrible thing to suffer like that at the end.

There was a lot to tell the authorities when we landed, I was certain they'd have questions.

Several times I heard Wren attempting the radio again, with no luck.

I wondered if it was safe to open the door, to step out. I wasn't taking a chance.

"Hey, guys," Will said calmly. "Is that another plane?"

Hearing that made me turn from the monitor.

Will was pointing to Wren's left and I stepped forward.

"Looks like it."

"Does it look like we're on the same path?" Will asked.

"He probably doesn't know we're here. He's above us."

I peered out, I could see the plane to our left. It was getting bigger and bigger.

"Shit," Wren blurted out. "He's coming fast."

"You said he was above us," Will said.

"Hold on." Wren grabbed the control wheel and pulled back.

I could feel the plane accelerating and I lost my balance falling back into Will as the plane made a rapid climb.

"Come on, come on," Wren beckoned.

My eyes stayed on that plane, it was coming toward us at full speed.

It suddenly turned to the right, and on its side, it began to drop.

Closer.

Closer. So close, another second, I would have seen the flight crew.

Wren lifted our plane within seconds of that plane smashing into us.

I swore it was going to catch us in its tailwind, if that was a thing. The vibration of the near miss caused our plane to shutter and shake. Controls and alarms blared and beeped.

"We're good. We're good," Wren said. His hands moving about the controls.

Like Will and Trace, my view went to the other window immediately to watch that plane.

It rotated and dropped like a missile. I couldn't see if it crashed, I could only assume it did.

Wren's exhale of relief was loud. "We're okay." His hands trembled slightly and all color had drawn from his face.

Though he tried not to show it, he was scared.

My heart raced, it was hard to breathe and I placed my hand on his shoulder. "Thank you."

Wren nodded.

"What the hell was that?" Trace asked.

"That plane was dead," Wren replied. "No power. No control. It was going down and we were in the way."

"How?"

Wren shook his head. "I don't know. But I'm starting to worry."

"About?" I asked.

"What's below."

"What do you mean?" I asked further.

"What if what happened to us, happened to them?" Wren suggested. "Only they couldn't see to control the plane."

"Like a mass terror attack," I guessed.

Trace looked back at me, then stood. He looked at the monitor then quietly opened the flight deck door.

Will whispered. "Where are you going?"

"To get that basket of booze," Trace answered. "I need it. We all may need it. I know what he's saying."

"What?" Will asked. "Wren, what does he mean?"

"No radio, no communication," Wren said. "After seeing that plane, I am starting to worry that what happened up here, happened everywhere. If I'm right, God help us when we land."

My entire soul cried out silently, "No." and I grabbed for the other seat and sat down.

I had fought the feeling that our plane wasn't an isolated incident.

I was still holding on to hope.

It had to be just us and maybe that other plane. It had to be.

I clutched to that belief, any other thoughts were far too much to bear.

CHAPTER NINE – THE GROUND

Sipping on another little bottle of vodka did little to calm my nerves. If it helped at all, it was more of a mental thing.

We fell into a wave of silence in that cockpit. The others, probably like me, worrying about the reality of what we faced.

Not that it was all fun and games. But before that plane almost slammed into us, it was more of a feeling that we survived this strange incident on the flight and when we landed all would be fine.

I'd call my family, probably be seen by a doctor, get interviewed by authorities.

But those thoughts were starting to wane.

They were replaced with a gut feeling that something more was terribly wrong.

I replayed that last conversation with my husband.

"Shelb, get home. Get home,"

I was so mad at him, thinking he was in some sort of jealous rage, I didn't ask why.

"No, listen to me …" he pleaded.

My son Alex, and my daughter Layla, all trying to get through to me.

But I wouldn't listen.

"Shelb, when you land you get on the next flight back."

Why didn't I listen?

Did he know something, had something already happened on the ground?

And then the connection was lost.

That part kept running over and over through my mind.

The static, the white screen, the tone.

My husband. My children.

Oh my God, my children.

What if it didn't happen on the ground? I needed to get to them. When we landed, I would be two thousand miles away.

No, no, no. I was wrong. I was thinking wrong. That gut feeling was fueled by worry not by fact. We didn't know.

I reasoned our situation. A mass terror attack on planes, that was it.

On the ground they were probably trying to track us, reach for us.

Sitting in that cockpit, tiny bottle of vodka in one hand, my phone in the other. I stared at my screen saver.

A picture of myself and my two children, smiling.

Layla was wearing her blue hoodie and Alex in his 'James Dean' look, I called it. White tee shirt and jeans. A statement. I never figured out what that statement was.

I loved them like any mother. Unconditionally and with every ounce of my soul.

They had to be okay.

They had to be. At any moment, Wren would tell us something.

I wasn't looking up, nor had I for at least the last twenty minutes of the flight.

"You okay?" Trace asked.

"I don't know," I replied. "I thought it was just us, you know. Now I'm not so sure."

"Whatever happened, if it isn't just us, we'll figure it out."

It was easy for him to say, his child was on the plane, alive and well with us. He knew the fate of the person he adored most in the world.

"Hey, guys," Wren's voice cracked as he spoke softly. 'This isn't good. Making our approach. We may want to prepare ourselves." He reached for the radio. "This is flight 1515, can you read us? We are making our approach."

Prepare ourselves.

Trace and Will looked out the window and finally, against what I wanted to do, I looked as well.

I had never flown to Las Vegas, but a co-worker told me to look out the window because as the plane approaches, you'll see the strip in all its glory.

My constant visits to the weather station predicted blue skies and hot temperatures.

There were no blue skies.

It was hard to see the skyline of the infamous strip.

A dark cloud hovered in the sky, streams of black smoke rising up fed that cloud as fires were burning on the ground.

And that was just what we saw in the distance.

That was just the strip.

There were so many spots of huge fires, it was as if we were on some volatile planet with eruptions of fire.

"What happened there?" Trace asked.

"Imagine," Will said. "Imagine if what happened up here happened down there at the same time. People dropped, if they were driving, they'd crash. Suddenly not being able to see or hear. That is what happened. All those fires out there, the big ones. Planes."

Wren said, "I think you're right."

I closed my eyes and sat back, downing that last little bit of Vodka in the bottle.

Trace asked. "Can we see any movement? Any traffic?"

"It's too smokey," answered Wren. "I'm circling around to the airport."

"Can you land?"

"I'll find a way. I have to. We need to get on the ground. I see a clear runway ahead."

Any time I ever flew before I always tuned in to the sound of the impending landing. Now, as I sat there, I didn't want to land. I didn't want to look, to face the truth.

It was dark and dismal on the ground. A quick glance up

as we made our way to the airport gave me the view of the terminal. It looked fine. For a split second I had some hope.

That was until we landed.

My eyes went to Wren, watching him.

The wheels touched down with the typical screech and the resistance as the plane fought to slow down.

We landed.

Wren brought the plane to a complete stop.

"Here's the deal," he said. "There's no communication, no jet bridge. I'll get us as close to the terminal as I can, but we'll have to get out using the emergency slide."

"What about those in the back?" Will asked.

"I don't know. We'll have to take a chance. I'll up the volume of the safety recording and we do it quietly," Wren said. "It doesn't look good."

"My God," Trace spoke softly. "What the hell?"

Finaly, I lifted my head and stood. The nose of the plane faced the airport. We didn't need to go inside or even get out of the plane to know that whatever happened on our plane, without a doubt, happened on the ground.

A yellow passenger plane had plowed into one of the terminals. The flames were out of control, releasing so much black smoke, and very little remained to burn. It was a shell. What we experienced was two hours earlier. It was hard to tell when it happened on the ground.

Wren taxied the plane slowly and closer to the terminal.

For as bad as things were on the plane, it was worse out there and I didn't want to leave.

Leaving meant facing the reality that my children, like those in Las Vegas, hadn't been spared.

CHAPTER TEN – FIRST DAY

I took my small backpack and purse with me when I left the plane. Little did Trace know I also dumped those bottles in my bag. I did it for him, because something told me he would physically need them. Not that I was an enabler but it wasn't the time for him to go sober and detox. I watched as he took several bottles from the flight attendant station as well.

When he claimed he was a professional, I realized how true that was. He had consumed more than I could, if I matched him, I'd be out cold. Even though he had some weight on me, he should have been acting drunk, he wasn't.

There was nothing fun about leaving the plane on the emergency slide. It was violent and not like the movies.

I didn't jump and slide, I old lady'ed it. Carefully crouching down, sitting on the edge and inching my way until the moment took hold.

It wasn't slow, it was fast and I panicked thinking I was going to fly off the end. I probably would have had Wren not been there waiting.

We exited quietly. Although when the door opened and the emergency slide was deployed, it caught the attention of those eight in the back of the plane.

Wren was ready for that. He had Will on the radio making loud noises and their attention was quickly turned away from our escape. They made it halfway to us, but that was it.

Those poor people would be stuck there.

I held on to zero hope that some sort of rescue awaited us.

We stood on what was called the tarmac, staring at the airport terminal.

Smoke from fires was hovering around what would have been a bright blue sky. It was exceptionally warm, way too hot.

There were four of us standing there in what I would call an apocalypse soundtrack. Slapping off flames, a distant moan or scream and otherwise silence. We didn't walk. We didn't move. We just stood there.

The airport didn't give us hope. Sporadic fires, a plane that had crashed into it. No emergency vehicles, no sirens. The backdrop of the airport was the iconic strip and from where I stood, it was no better than the airport. It spelled out to me nothing less than chaos and death.

Immediately I pulled out my phone and called home. Maybe it was just the plane that stopped me from making contact.

Ring after ring, then finally voicemail.

I tried my husband, my children, my sister.

I tried everyone.

No answers.

My hands shook and my soul trembled just as badly. I could feel it deep in me, the worry, the fear, the unconfirmed notion that things in our world had just taken a nosedive.

"What now?" asked Will. "I mean. What do we do?"

Trace answered. "I don't know, I really didn't think too far past getting on the ground."

"We need to know," Wren said. "Are things bad everywhere. I mean, we're standing out here looking, but things might be different inside.'

"Or they may not be," Trace said.

I held up my phone. "My family isn't answering. What am I supposed to do?"

"Listen," Wren faced me. "No matter what the situation, we will find a plane, I'll get you home. I promise. Right now." His head turned toward the airport. "We need to know what is happening, we need some sort of answers, and going in there is the only way to find that out."

"We survived this," Will stated. "By being in the bathroom. He survived by sleeping. There have to be people like us and … we don't know if it is global. We don't."

"The only one way to find out," Trace said. "Let's head inside."

Maybe it was because we still were a good distance away, but it took until we neared the building to see the bodies on the ground.

Just laying there.

It hurt my soul. I felt it when I saw them.

Workers just doing their job, lay where they fell. Six or seven bodies. Two were near a plane, loading luggage.

We pushed forward.

It wasn't like there was a stairway to the terminal, we entered the bottom floor. It looked like a factory with conveyor belts. No luggage moved on it. I supposed the luggage loaded before the incident had already arrived where it needed to go.

There were more dead bodies inside, but also those like Mary. Standing, moving in circles feeling their way about, some sat on the ground.

We were quiet, we didn't say a word, we didn't know if anyone in that luggage area was like the eight on the plane.

Maybe the ones on the plane were just a fluke.

One thing was clear, the airport, at least the behind the scenes luggage area were like the plane.

There were no answers there, only more confusion and questions in my mind. Will pointed to a door, he did some sort of sign language to Trace and Trace nodded.

He faced me and Wren mouthing the word exit.

Exit to where?

We made our way there and the double doors led down a hall.

A time clock was there, a break room on the right, we kept on walking.

At the end of the hall was another set of double doors.

Trace paused before opening them. "This is baggage claim

and pick up. I can't promise what's out here," he spoke softly. "Just stay quiet."

"What if it's more of the same?" I asked. "There's no answers in more of the same."

Wren replied. "Then we leave to look for answers."

I groaned softly. "My family. I need to find out about my family."

"You're four hours away from your family," Trace said. "It's not like they're down the street. We find out what's happening. We take a moment and try to figure things out and when we do, we can come back."

"Lots of planes here," said Wren. "I can get you back. But I do think we should wait a few hours, maybe eight."

"Why?" I asked.

"We don't need a repeat of what happened in the air," Wren said. "We wait. If this is global and planes are dropping from the sky, right now … there's an average of nine thousand, seven hundred planes in the sky. That's a lot of planes to fall."

Like bombs.

It was a big country, but still how many planes flew into Las Vegas? How many were in the air?

"Granted," Wren continued, "They'll more than likely continue to fly until they run out of fuel. That is why I want to wait. Let's do this."

We walked through those doors and came to a stairwell that led down and up.

We chose down.

No people. No workers. No bodies.

Before going to Las Vegas. I had a friend that had been there many times. She said to me that while walking through the casino what I needed to listen for.

There will be three sounds.

Silence.

Music from the slot machines.

Or winning music.

I didn't know what winning music was, I really didn't. But I was sure it wasn't playing when we passed through those double doors of the luggage area.

There certainly was music. Tinkles of tunes here and there, but for the most part it was silent.

We emerged by one of those massive coffee chain spots and into the luggage claim area.

Stores to the right, people had just dropped. The luggage moved about the carousel, round and round and no one claimed them.

We walked by the luggage claim and saw several people on the belt, moving with the luggage.

I didn't see anyone walking, moving, crying or struggling.

I didn't see anything like the eight from the plane.

Trace led the way, as if he had been there before.

I really tried not to look.

I didn't want to, my heart broke for those people and for every fallen person I saw, I thought about my family.

On a mission we walked straight for the exit doors which led outside.

The heat blasted us once again and now I was met with silence.

Cars had crashed into each other, bodies remained in the cars. There was a long line of taxis, smashed bumper to bumper as people lay on the sidewalk with their luggage.

"This way." Wren pointed and walked away from the line of taxis.

We had made it through the baggage claim, but not far into our walk down the line of Taxi cabs, I saw people.

They wandered aimlessly, moving left to right. Calling out in an uninterpretable way, words I couldn't understand.

I felt horrible for them.

Were they like Mary, unable to see or hear? Or were they like the eight?

To suddenly lose that ability was unfathomable.

I couldn't even comprehend what they were going through.

I only hoped and prayed that they didn't either. That when

they lost those senses, they lost something else, the ability to realize what happened.

Thrust into darkness and silence.

Feeling the impact of a crash, not knowing what happened. Hoping anyone would help.

Were we wrong for not helping?

Was it our moral duty to help them?

Were there too many to help? What could we do?

We wandered through the heat that beat against us, following Wren.

He checked each and every car and van we passed, then finally he stopped.

"This one," he said, pointing to a white van taxi. He opened the driver's seat and reached inside.

There was a man inside, a driver. I turned my head as Wren pulled him out.

I didn't want to look, I didn't even know what he did with the body. Once he gave us the okay, I went to the passenger's side and got it.

It was hot and stale and smelled in the van like body odor and urine. I covered my nose.

Wren got in and took his place in the driver's seat. His hands stayed on the wheel for a while and he stared out.

"Why this one?" Trace asked.

"He turned off the engine. He probably was just giving it a break waiting for his turn to go ahead." Wren replied and started the van. "We have half a tank. Give it a second, it will cool down."

"Obviously, you know Las Vegas," I said.

"I've been here a few times."

"Me, too," said Trace. "I think we need to head downtown."

"That's what I thought," Wren replied. "The police, courthouse, all of that is downtown."

I didn't know Las Vegas. Downtown to me was where that pyramid was. I would soon learn that was wrong.

"Let's do this." Wren put the van in gear and carefully pulled out.

I was sitting next to Will. The young man that was always vocal now was suddenly quiet. His fingers tapped against each other as he kept his hands in a prayer fashion.

"Are you okay?" I asked Will.

"No. No I'm not," Will replied. "I keep thinking of everything. How this was an ordinary day, taking a flight, headed to my grandmother's. Many times, we landed in Las Vegas, to see Gram. You know? Get off the flight, get our bags, stand at the taxi station. It moved like a well-greased wheel. But now …. it's different. Everything is still. Everything is dead. Everything is surreal."

"I know," I replied.

"What are we hoping to find?" he asked. "Answers to what happened? As if some police station out there is operational and some guy behind a desk will give us answers. The world ended while we were thirty thousand feet in the air."

"It didn't end," Trace looked back from the front seat. "The world didn't end. It just had some sort of event. Something happened. And we need to find out what that was."

"It may be just in some places," I said. "God, I hope it was only in some places."

"We'll find that out," Trace said. "We're on the ground, we're safe. We'll find answers."

CHAPTER ELEVEN – NOT MY VEGAS

The four of us were in that van. Honestly, I didn't know where I was going. Wren and Grace both stated that downtown was the place to go. I didn't know what was downtown, I had never been to Las Vegas before.

But we didn't drive for long, or in my opinion make really any distance.

A few minutes into our drive we eventually had to stop. Traffic was backed up, no way around the cars that were on the freeway.

When the event happened, it rendered everyone incapacitated and if they were driving, they just crashed.

One moment driving at a high rate of speed, the next unable to see or hear.

For someone like me, it was hard to imagine.

I likened it to the sun.

Driving at a bad time, when the sun blared through the windshield blinding me. In a slightly panicked mode, looking to my right for the safety lines and trying to find them with the sun in my way. To navigate blindly.

I never understood why car manufacturers didn't do the same with windshields that eyeglass makers did. Progressive lenses, darkening with the light.

But the sun at the wrong time took my ability to see. I imagined those driving at the moment of the event felt the same.

They weren't as fortunate.

Their ability to see didn't return.

And what was the event?

What happened in a snap that caused all of it?

We navigated around most of the crashed vehicles for at least a couple miles, then we couldn't.

We had to stop, pull over and walk.

We were on a freeway, a highway of sorts. An elevated roadway. Multitudes of cars everywhere.

When we were finally unable to drive farther, we faced a wall of cars.

All fender benders.

The drivers of the vehicles slumped over at the wheel.

More had died from the event than had lived with the blinding and deaf disabilities.

On that freeway overpass it was silent, quiet, with no movement.

Whatever happened occurred hours earlier. The car alarms were silent with cars now having dead batteries.

Car after car, vans and trucks, abandoned.

"We have about two miles," said Wren. "We have to walk."

Walk to where?

Where could we possibly walk that would give us any answers?

All around us was death. Really was there a place in Las Vegas unscathed, untouched, where first responders were gathering people and helping them?

In Wren's mind is that what he believed or hoped?

More than anything I wanted to believe that, but I knew, we faced something unfathomable. I couldn't process it. It was like a movie. A scary movie with a happy ending.

In reality there was no happy ending.

I just wanted to go home.

I didn't say anything, I just walked, following their lead, carrying my purse and backpack. The heat was nearly unbearable.

The reality of all those bodies baking in the Las Vegas sun was not lost to me. I knew in hours, not days, how bad things would be.

I could already smell the hint of decay that filled the air.

I just wanted to go home.

It was like being out with friends on a bad night, thinking of home and how much better it would be just to be there.

The more I passed the cars and saw the bodies, the more I knew that if it was everywhere, that second I dismissed my husband and the screen went white, was the moment I lost my family.

I was beyond pain. An aching, seething pain of grief and fear for my children, my husband, my family.

What would I do? How would I go on? If by God, something happened to them, what would my next course of action be? That was my thought process as I walked, that was where my mind was. Not on finding answers to the world problem. But finding answers to my family.

I tried.

With half of my battery power remaining on my phone, I kept trying to contact my family and friends. Anyone I knew.

Even work colleagues. I called, texted, everything as I walked.

There was no response,

Despite having a direction or an end goal, the four of us moved aimlessly.

No water. No food.

One step at a time.

My body felt on fire and my lips were dry. I kept trying to moisten them, but it didn't help.

At what point would we say, what is next?

We followed Wren.

Everything was the same. Nothing had changed. Cars. Bodies. Silence. A long walk only to turn back around and head back to the airport? Why didn't we just stay at the airport, wait out Wren's time frame for danger. It was insane that we were walking and looking for answers.

An endless field of death with no light at the end of the tunnel.

After an hour, we arrived at the Clark County Municipal building.

We stood outside of it, looking.

"This is a bust," Trace said. "No one is alive here."

"We have to try," said Wren as he stepped through the door.

Trace followed, then Will. But Will stopped when he noticed I wasn't moving.

"Are you coming? Will asked.

"No," I replied. "I'll wait here. Go on."

"It'll be cooler in there," Will said. "The AC is still running."

"I know. Go on. I'll be okay."

When the three of them went into the building, I sat down on the concrete steps. Let them go, let them see there was no news to find out.

Only death. Everything was dead.

Sitting there, it was the first time the heat didn't bother me. I just stared out.

Maybe they'd try a radio or phone. Or perhaps put on a television. Whatever they'd find out they'd tell me.

I opened up my backpack and pulled out one of those tiny airplane bottles of booze. I was well aware that alcohol didn't help dehydration, but I was thirsty and I downed one.

It wet my mouth and gave me a moment of relief from the dry hot air.

I looked out at the streets, the cars and vehicles, the bodies everywhere.

No one wandered or walked about like they did at the airport.

Maybe being inside when the event happened was a way to survive, even if it came with the cost of losing the precious senses of sight and sound.

Inside was where I saw the survivors.

The airport, the plane.

And what would I do next? What would I do if the unthinkable had happened? My family gone.

Would I just die?

Live and help others or live and be alone?

So many thoughts entered my mind as I sat there waiting for Wren, Will and Trace.

Was it really the end of the world? Or perhaps it was just a portion of America that had come under attack?

Sitting there, sipping the last of that little bottle, I heard the voice.

"Are you real?" the woman's voice asked.

The tiny bottle lowered from my lips with a popping suctioning sound and I looked out and to my left.

She walked slowly down the sidewalk.

A woman, around my age.

"Please tell me you're real."

I stood. "I am."

She groaned out a sob of relief and ran to me.

Instinctively, I hurried down the steps as if greeting an old friend.

The woman grabbed on to me and embraced me tightly.

"Someone else is alive and okay. Thank God."

"I'm alive," I said. "And okay. Others are, too. They're inside the police station. Trying to find out what happened."

The woman began to cry. "I've been walking and looking at everyone."

"You found us." I placed my hands on her shoulders.

"Us?" she asked.

"Us," I replied. "Me and three others."

"Thank God."

"Do you know what happened?"

She shook her head. "I was getting an MRI. For my hip. I was getting one, listening to music and it was taking a while. I thought something was wrong and I screamed and screamed and hit the button." Her head lowered. "They were …. something was wrong with them. They were crying out. Reaching out."

"Who?" I asked.

"The people at the clinic."

"They're alive?"

She nodded. "But something was wrong, like they couldn't hear me or see me. When I came outside, everyone was dead. Cars crashed. I can't reach my children."

"Me either. But you don't know what happened?"

Again, she shook her head. "Do you?"

"No. We were on a plane. We landed. It's only us. Are you from here?"

"Yes. I live a few miles from here."

"Why didn't you go home?" I asked. "If I was close to my family, I would try to go home."

"That's where I'm headed and I saw you. I'm scared. I'm scared to go home. No one is answering."

I embraced the woman in comradery. "I hear that. If you live that close, I can go with you."

"Will you?"

I nodded and turned back toward the door of the police station. "I will."

"Do you think this is just Las Vegas?"

"I don't know. But maybe this is over. Maybe whatever happened didn't happen everywhere. We need to find out."

"We do. I'm scared."

"Me, too. Let me get the others."

In that moment, seeing the woman, whose name I had not learned, filled me with a renewed hope.

She was alive,

Others would be, too.

There was a chance my children, my family wasn't hurt. Maybe they were watching the news waiting to hear about me.

As I made my attempt to go back into the police station, I heard it. A high pitch whistling sound.

Both her and I stopped and looked back, looked around for the sound.

I knew what it was and I didn't want to admit it.

It grew louder and louder and as my head raised in the direction of the sound, I saw it.

A plane.

It was so low, so close to us. Upside down it glided in a downward spiral.

There were no engines noises, just the sound of the plane falling from the sky. Whistling in the wind as it made its free fall, final descent.

Wren spoke of it happening.

No one alive to fly the plane.

Running out of fuel and dropping from the sky.

Like a missile it made its arrival and within seconds it landed.

Or rather crashed.

The ground vibrated and shook and an explosion rang out.

I saw the fireball consume the western sky.

I clutched the woman, a stranger, closing my eyes tightly.

It wasn't happening, it couldn't be happening.

Another plane fell, like the one that almost hit us.

For as much as I wanted to believe all that was happening wasn't real or wasn't global, the sight of that plane crashing was a harsh reality I wasn't ready to face.

CHAPTER TWELVE – TAKING THE LEAD

I wouldn't have imagined I would have been so close to a plane crashing, yet there I was. I lost my footing on those stairs from the quaking ground, the fireball consumed the skyline and I felt the blast of heat.

I watched it fall from the sky, the belly of the plane so close I swore I could touch it.

It didn't take long for Trace, Will and Wren to come racing from the police station.

"Are you alright?" Trace asked, then his eyes went to the woman.

"We're fine," I replied. "We were coming to get you. This is …"

"Emily," the woman replied. "Emily."

I pointed out everyone, giving their names, then explained to them it was another plane that fell.

"That's what I was saying," Wren said. "We need to wait."

"She wants to go home," I explained. "She lives nearby. I said I'd go with her. If we're waiting to leave, then there's no harm in going."

"I agree," added Trace. "It won't hurt and maybe we can find answers."

"Really?" I snapped. "There are no answers. We're wasting time looking for them."

"What do you suggest we do?" asked Trace.

"Help where we can, like with Emily."

"That's what we'll do then." Trace nodded. "Emily, can you

lead the way?"

Emily nodded nervously and stepped from the stairs of the police station. She started walking, looking back to make sure we were still behind her and staying close.

Will grabbed my arm to get my attention. "Do we know how she survived without being blind, losing her hearing or mind."

"She was getting an MRI."

"Eyes and ears protected again," said Will. "It had to hit the brain by those means of transmission. Sound and light. But what was it?"

"And do you think we'll find out," I said as we walked. "We won't. Anyone that could know is gone. The only answers I want are about my family."

As the heat increased so did my thirst. I wish I would have thought of it, but it didn't cross my mind after watching that plane.

With each step I walked my lips felt like sandpaper. It was hard to focus on what was around me, the cars that had smashed into each other and into buildings.

Still, there were no people wandering. Not like Emily, not like the ones in the airport or any like Mary.

"Another block," Emily said, moving quickly and with purpose. "I promise."

We passed a bookstore, but nowhere in our six-block walk had I seen a convenience store or coffee shop. There was a wedding chapel in the distance.

"Did you walk to the MRI?" I asked.

"No, I drove, but someone smashed into my car and I couldn't drive it," she replied.

Will trotted to catch up to her. "Have you seen anyone that was affected by the event?"

"You mean the people with the eyes?" Emily asked. "Yes. At the clinic. I felt horrible leaving, so many people, crying and reaching out. There weren't enough hands to help them."

"As in people that survive unscathed?" Will asked.

"Yes."

Trace questioned. "What were they doing when the event happened."

"I do know, some people could see, but they couldn't hear. It's so strange."

"But hopefully," Wren said. "I mean, not everyone is dead. So, it's hopeful.' He looked at me. "I know you made the comment about getting answers, but there has to be some out there. I think I may know where."

"Where?" I asked.

"Nellis Air Force Base," Wren replied.

"That's not far," Emily said. "About ten miles."

"What about getting me home?" I asked.

"I will get you there."

Emily stopped after she turned a corner. "There. I live there." She pointed to the house second from the corner.

At first, I wondered why she didn't rush to it. Desperately running in to see if her family was alright, then it hit me. She was scared, I would be, too. Like opening a letter, you knew could contain something bad.

Not wanting to see it but holding on to hope instead. She stood there staring at the home, still not on the property. Afraid to get close.

I would be the same way and probably will when I went home.

Trace stepped forward. "Would you like me to go and check first?"

"No. But I'd like you to walk in with me, please."

"You got it."

Her pace, which had been brisk now slowed down as we made it to her front walk.

"What's that sound?" Will asked.

For a second it didn't register what he was talking about, then I heard. A beeping.

"Shit." Trace ran up the walkway. "That's the smoke alarm."

Emily picked up her pace again as Trace opened the front door. When he did, I could see the smoke lingering and making its escape through the open doorway.

It wasn't black smoke.

Emily charged in calling out for her husband and children. Crying out their names over and over as she moved quickly about the house in search of them.

When I arrived inside, I could see Trace in front of the open oven. He tossed a pan in the sink. "It could have been worse. Grabbing a broom, he searched for the squealing alarm to silence it.

"Is it out?" Wren asked.

"Yeah. No one is in this kitchen," Trace replied.

"Where are they?" Emily raced back into the living room. "Where are they? They aren't here."

"Emily." Will called her name softly.

When I heard how he summoned her, I worried. A knot formed in the pit of my stomach. I saw it on her face, too, as the color drained in her fear.

Will pointed out the window. "Is that them?"

Emily looked quickly and without hesitating ran out the back door.

Her family was there. Huddled together. Her husband held the two boys close to him.

They were alive, but I could tell they were affected. Even at a distance, I could see their eyes.

CHAPTER THIRTEEN – REST BEFORE GOING

How horrible it had to be for her husband, Baily. To know he couldn't see or hear his children cry but smell the burning food in the oven and take them outside to safety. The desperation he must have felt. As a mother I understood that.

I helped her gather her family and lead them to the backyard furniture.

It was so hot outside, to me they couldn't stay there for long.

But Emily insisted at least for a little bit.

Baily tried to speak, his words were jumbled, once or twice a word would come out that I could understand, but for the most part, it was like he was trying to sing along with a song he didn't know the words to. That's what he sounded like.

Like Mary.

She stayed outside with him and I went back inside to help Trace get the house in order.

Wren and Will left to see if they could find a path to the freeway. A street that was blocked with wreckage.

I finally got my water and downed most of the bottle without stopping.

Looking around the house, I could see when it happened.

A children's streaming channel played videos, toys were on the ground, the coffee table was toppled over, as were the dining room chairs.

Baily knew his home well enough to make his way out.

When it happened and he lost his sight and ability to hear, I don't know how he found his children. But he did.

I straightened up the living room and grabbed the remote control, looking at it, I realized, Emily's family, like mine, gave up traditional cable.

Any chance for the news would be lost.

"All good?" Trace came into the living room.

"No cable."

"Hit the 'home' button and pick live TV."

"Really?"

"You didn't know that?"

I shook my head. And did as he said, locating the Live TV, but hesitant to press it.

"What's wrong?"

"What if nothing is there?"

"What if that's not the case?" Trace took the remote and aimed it.

The channels with news weren't major networks.

They were little stations trying to look big. The first one showed an empty desk, the second channel he found only had an image, and the third, we could hear sounds, but didn't see anything.

He placed down the remote. "Maybe Nellis will have answers."

"I can't believe this is happening." I sat down on the couch and took a drink of my water. "What was burning?"

"I'm sorry."

"What was he baking that it took several hours to start to burn?"

"I think a meatloaf."

"In the morning?" I asked.

"Maybe he was making her lunch."

I sighed out. "How did he do what he did? He found his kids and got them out."

"Wouldn't you?"

"Yeah, I'd try." I finished my water and stood up again. "You said your grandmother was deaf."

"My mother, Will's grandmother," he replied.

"Was she born deaf?"

"No, she lost her hearing in an accident when she was ten."

"So she spoke."

Trace nodded. "Yeah, when she signed, she spoke a lot."

"Why can't they speak?" I asked. "I mean you're a doctor, they have the ability to be vocal, but, maybe it's my ignorance, even unable to hear themselves, they'd talk, right?"

"Are you talking about how Baily sounds?"

"Yes."

"I listened. It sounds to me like Apraxia of speech."

"What is that?" I asked.

"It's when the brain knows what it wants to say, but as it sends the signal to the vocal chords it gets jumbled. What the brain wants to say isn't what comes out. The blessing is he can't hear that he's not saying what he wants."

"So, it affected, eyes, ears and brain."

"Left side, and in some … it looks like causes behavioral issues. But likely, we only ran into those on the plane."

I shook my head. "So many dead."

"We don't know how far it has spread or where it is all happening. We are the mercy of a world with vacant technology."

"What do you mean?"

"We have lights. We have internet, but no one is able to give us anything."

"That's not promising." I walked to the dining room and looked out the window. "It's so hot out there, can't you get them to come in."

"I will."

"Can you imagine how many people are affected like this. How many mothers and fathers were with their children, trying to find them. Crying babies with no one to hold them."

"That will change." Trace stood next to me.

"You think they'll get their sight and hearing back."

"I don't know, but if they don't, it will change. The human

spirit is amazing and adaptable. Give it a week or so to adjust and they'll find a way to get about. To live, to eat, survive and communicate. Those affected will learn. The lucky ones will be the ones that have someone to help them."

"Do you think that's our moral obligation?"

"What? To help them?" Trace shrugged. "I gave up on the religious aspect of life a while ago. But I think after we get our priorities in order, then, yes, maybe."

"What are your priorities?" I asked him.

"My son. And if he says let's help those people, then that's what we do. However … if we help them, they'll never help themselves."

"That's horrible."

"Is it?" Trace asked. "If this is what life handed them right now, and this is the way they have to be for the rest of their life, then if we do their day to day lives, then they won't survive without us. We need to teach them to live."

I glanced out at Emily and her family. "If I find my husband and children like this, then I will be like Emily. Taking care of them."

"Her husband already proved he can survive without someone showing him. I am willing to bet that man out there, in a few months' time will be just fine. Back to baking a meatloaf. And had Emily not come home, he would have made sure his children survived."

"You're optimistic."

"I know the spirit of people. And … I also know what the body can tolerate."

"What do you mean?"

"I'm bringing that family in from the heat. I want to talk to Emily to make sure she has everything she needs and we figure out a way for her to communicate with him before we leave. She has the bigger task."

Trace was thinking farther ahead than the immediate circumstances. I wish I could.

"I think she'll be fine," I said. "I would be."

"Of course," Trace said. "If this is it."

I stammered my words some in questioning what he meant. "What ... this is it, right?"

"Is it?" Trace asked as he walked to the kitchen door. "If this is a terror attack or some sort of isolated accident, then yeah. But what if it's more? What if all this is just the start to something bigger."

He walked to the back door and out, leaving me hanging on those final words.

Bigger?

People lost their sight, their ability to hear, to speak. So many people died, some lost their minds.

It had to be all because I couldn't fathom what else could happen that could be bigger.

CHAPTER FOURTEEN – THE WAY

There was an overwhelming sense that she did not want us to leave. That she was scared and didn't want to be alone with her husband and children out of fear. Who could blame her? Her neighborhood was quiet. There were dead all around. I hated the thought of leaving her. I really did. We stayed long enough at her home and had to make our way to Nellis Air Force Base. We made sure she had everything she needed and while the cell phones were still operational, we gave her our numbers. I didn't know what else to do. None of us did. The poor woman was left alone to care for her family. I felt it was a grave error on our part, leaving, that maybe we should have extended an invitation or at least, perhaps we came back after we found anything out.

How terrifying it had to be for her. When she needed food, how would she get it? Sure, the grocery stores are plentiful, at the very least she could take from the neighbors, but for the time being she had to take care of her kids. They at least knew how to communicate.

Trace was an amazing help with that. He was teaching her how to communicate, using touch. Her fingers to their hand. He started with water.

It would have to be every day training and learning again.

I hated walking out that door. I kept looking back at her, controlling my pitiful glance and how sorry I felt and imagining that could be me.

We used a neighbor's car and navigated some of the

Backstreets, thankfully we waited until Five PM when the sun was starting to go down a little. It was still hot and Las Vegas was so unbelievably hot. Once we hit the freeway things began to congest. We weaved in and out cautiously for a while, and then we had to stop and abandon the car.

Two miles. We had two miles to walk. Will joked that the strip was five point eight miles and he had walked it several times, which didn't help me. I didn't know what we would find or why we were even going to the Air Force base.

I just wanted to go home. Wren promised me he would take me home. Maybe it was selfish of me. I charged my phone at Emily's home and kept trying to reach my family, but if they were like her family, they would never hear the phone ring. Would they be able to eat or drink? Would they survive until I got there?

My guilt for leaving Emily stayed with me. I mean, what if that was me? What would I do? Would I willingly stay home or would I beg to go? She probably didn't wanna be a burden. But that weight of guilt was far too much.

"I think we should go back," I said. "Not right now, but after we're done and before we leave. We shouldn't leave them behind if they had neighbors that would be one thing, but they don't. She's alone and it's a lot to deal with alone. "

Wren looked over me and said, "I had every intention of going back. We need to stick together because we're going to find our families and similar situations. I hope not, but chances are we will. We are abandoning no one, but it would have been too much to take them all on this particular trip to the Air Force Base."

Neither Trace nor Will disagreed, they just kept walking along with me. I felt better. These were good men with me. Why would I think they wouldn't want to go back and help Emily? We screwed up with Mary whether intentional or not, and I wasn't taking that chance with Emily.

How much more time would it add to my getting home? A few hours?

"Did you tell her?" I asked Wren. "Maybe I should call her and tell her we'll be back."

Trace replied, "That's a good idea."

"When will that be though?" I asked Will.

Wren replied, "Well, depending on what we find at Nellis. It could be a few hours tops. At the latest tomorrow and before you say anything," he pointed at me. "I promised I'd get you home to Cleveland and I will. I will. I appreciate you waiting."

"You said eight hours. it's been just that and another plane hasn't fallen from the sky. Here a few hours more isn't going to hurt." I lifted my phone from my pocket. Emily's number was already programmed in, and I called her. She didn't answer. I left the voicemail and I followed it with a text. Both saying the same thing, "After we find out, if we find out anything at Nellis, we will be back. We wanted to take you guys with us. Get back to me."

There was no response, but I was sure she had her hands full and would get back eventually.

* * *

It wasn't what I expected. Actually, I didn't know what to expect.

Would the final leg of the journey be more of the same? Roadways littered with crashed cars and abandoned vehicles. The bodies of those who now succumbed to the heat because they could walk to get help.

Lost in their own silence and darkness, feeling the heat eating against them.

The backdrop of the setting sun gave me an eerie sense we were just wandering and walking into more of the same.

Wren had given us a heads up that it was heavily guarded

and wouldn't be easy to get into.

As we finally approached the gate, my body beaten down by the heat and exhaustion, I saw the base sign, lit by spotlights. Next to it, parked sideways and blocking the gate, was a truck.

I figured we would be walking right in.

Until a spotlight hit us.

"Stop."

We did. About twenty feet from the truck.

"Are you guys alright? Okay?" said a male voice.

"We're fine. All of us are fine," Wren replied. "We're survivors. We were on a plane. Would Colonel Simpson be here? He can vouch for me. I'm Captain Wren Lockheart."

"Sorry, sir," the male voice replied. "The Colonel was a casualty of the event." The young man in uniform lifted a radio. "Ma'am, we have survivors that made it here."

"How many?" she replied.

"Four. They look like they've been walking awhile."

"Bring them in, please. Let's get them taken care of."

"Yes, Ma'am. One of them identified himself as Captain Wren Lockheart, he asked for Colonel Simpson."

"Please tell him that Colonel Higgins will be happy to greet him."

"Come in. I'll take you to the colonel."

"Higgins?" Wren asked. "Mallory Higgins?"

"Yes, sir," the soldier answered.

I caught up to Wren. "Do you know her?"

"I do. If anyone has answers, she does."

The young soldier took us to a jeep just inside the gate, we got inside.

I sat in the back between Trace and Will as the jeep drove off.

Trace caught me looking at my phone.

"Did she get back to you?" he asked. "Emily, I mean."

"No." I shook my head.

"I'm sure she is fine. She has a lot going on."

"Yeah, she does." I glanced up to the sky, it was getting darker by the minute. How long had we walked, it had been most of the day that we landed in Las Vegas and I hadn't eaten a thing.

Settling in that jeep, I felt my stomach rumble from hunger and my lips were drying out more from thirst.

I kept telling myself I was better off than so many people.

I just wanted to get home, and though the others sought answers to what happened, I really just wanted to know about my family.

The staunch and stronger looking woman with red and gray short hair in uniform, was already in the lobby of the visitor's center waiting on us when we walked in. It was large and open and very few lights were on.

"Captain,' she said with a smile.

"Ma'am," he snapped to attention, then after they shook hands.

"Were you with the president?"

"No ma'am, I was on a civilian flight to Vegas. As were these folks here." He indicated to our group.

"How did that go?" she asked.

Wren shook his head. "We're the ones that got off. I landed the plane at the airport and we made our way here."

"So, you got a look around?"

"We did. Do you know what's happening?" Wren asked.

"We're piecing it together," she replied.

"Is it everywhere?" I asked.

"I'm afraid it looks like it," she answered.

My head lowered and I felt a comforting hand lightly rub my back for support. It was Trace.

Trace spoke up. "Is it the same as here? Mixed effects on different people? We're seeing different things. Some people deaf and blind, some dead ..."

"Us, as well," she said.

Wren added. "Trace is a doctor."

"Oh, wonderful. We lost both our base doctors. Please." She stepped back, motioning her hand. "Let's get you something to eat and drink and we can talk."

Mallory turned and led the way across the darkened visiting center.

Trace whispered to me. "I know you're worried. I know you don't care about answers. But the more information you have when you go home the better."

I didn't verbally respond. I got what he was saying.

But what more could she tell us? At that point in time, I didn't care what happened, because it happened.

And whatever was the outcome it was all the same, and we had to face it.

CHAPTER FIFTEEN – SOME NEWS

The mood was somber. How could it not be? Everyone we walked by looked like we did, lost, desperate, and sad.

Mallory led us into a big room with tables, the food court. A table was set up with coffee and sandwiches. I knew I was hungry, but didn't realize how badly I needed to eat until I took a bite of the sandwich.

I did keep checking my phone.

"They won't reply," said Mallory. "Most who survived can't hear or see."

Trace asked, "Have you examined the ones on base that can't hear or see to find out medically what happened?"

"We don't have the equipment to do so, but we will," Mallory replied. "There was a man in Arizona that contacted us by radio and said he was going to try to do that.

"They're going to have to be fast," said Trace. "Power will go down with no one manning the stations."

"I told him that. Right now, we need to find people like us, they're out there."

"I know," I said. "We met a woman who was like us, but her family was affected. We left her behind to come here. I'm just worried about her."

"That's sad."

Trace leaned onto the table. "Have you run across anyone that seemed violent. I'm sure they only hear, they can't see, and they attack."

"No." Mallory shook her head. "No one here."

Trace sat back. "Maybe it had something to do with being on a plane."

"That information," Mallory said. "Will be helpful. We're trying to pull it all together with experts that survived."

"So, there are experts alive?" Will asked.

"A few," answered Mallory. "Not here. We lost sixty percent of those on base. Dead instantly. Another ten percent were rendered deaf and blind. We're still grappling with that."

Wren questioned, "Have you heard from anyone else about what might have happened?"

"It's still early. We're still gathering information. It appears you may have already figured this out, that whatever occurred through an oscular and aural means simultaneously. Both are an entry for brain disturbance or damage. Those it didn't kill, it blinded them and took away their ability to hear."

Trace nodded. "We figured as much."

"And those who survived unscathed like us were in protected areas. Underground, in a place with no outdoor lights, or their eyes blocked, also wearing headphones."

"So, all those people taking the subway," Will said with optimism. "They may have survived. It was rush hour on the East coast."

I sputtered out. "One point two million people ride the New York subway during rush hour. If ten percent of those were underground when it happened that's a hundred thousand healthy people." I then noticed Trace looking at me.

"Nothing. It's just the second time you have a really specific statistic."

"I like statistics."

Mallory asked. "Are you a mathematician?"

"No, a loan processor for a discount furniture store. I just like stats."

"I think it's cool," Will said. "And knowing that a lot could have survived is good news."

"Is it?" Wren asked. "This is a chaos enduring situation."

"I have faith in humanity," I said.

Trace spoke again, "So we don't know any more than that?"

"Not at this time." Mallory sighed out. "Unfortunately, those of us who did survive have no idea what the event entailed except it was something visual and audible."

When she said that something clicked inside of me. My mind flashed back to that moment in the airplane bathroom. Arguing with my husband or rather not listening to his moaning. Audible.

Visual

Could it be that I saw?

"I … I think I know "I said. "I was on the phone with my husband or rather a video message. When it happened "

"So, you saw something?" asked Mallory "Something that happened?

"Yes. I think. Right before the plane dropped, I lost connection with my husband. The entire screen of the phone whited out. I'm sorry not the entire screen just the video portion. I thought it was on because I could still see the effect parts and the camera thing to turn it around all that stuff whatever you call it. I could still see it, but where he was whited out as if it was … "

"Like a nuclear flash?" Trace asked.

"Yes, yes that's it. It whites out and then. There was a feedback sound." I added. "It can't be a coincidence. It has to be it. I didn't think much of it at the time but, audible and visual. Yes, it has to be it, right?"

Mallory knotted. "This is good information right now we're gathering everything we can. The flash, the sound, now figuring that with the seismic activity."

All of us had a shocked look on our faces when she said that.

Wren asked, "I'm sorry, seismic activity?"

"Yes, lots of it," Mallory replied. "The last four hours up and down the East coast and Southern Midwest like Texas, New Orleans. Oddly enough we find this out by intercepting radio transmissions. Once we learned of it, we started planning teams to go out and check."

"The radio transmissions," I said. "They weren't military."

"No. Not at all."

Mallory paused and sipped her coffee. "Some religious radio station. They're calling it Gods end, and now just thinking about it, something else makes sense. The bright white light and the sound."

Wren muttered, "And a bright light from Heaven flashed around Saul. He was blinded. Acts Nine or something like that."

Mallory added. "And then came the high pitch sound breaking glass and causing him to fall to his knees."

Wren looked at her curiously. "What?"

"I'm just adding," she said. "That was from Supernatural season four episode one. When Castiel tries to speak to Dean."

I sat back. "So, this is where they think it's Gods end?"

"The angels have come," she said. "Now the sky will fall and the earth will quake. If prophecy is right."

"Do you believe that?" I asked.

She shook her head. "That's the prophecy. No. But it's something. And more is definitely coming."

* * *

There were no planes they could spare to get me home, but they would get us close to the car first thing in the morning. I hated it, I really did. I wanted to go home, but I understood the reason why I had to wait.

There was no way to know what was happening out there in the dark, desolate streets. We still couldn't confirm if the violent behavior was only on the plane, or if it was everywhere.

It wasn't really dark.

There was an explanation for it.

Mallory said because power was supplied by the Hoover Dam, they'd have electricity longer than anyone else in the country.

I was given a small room to rest and sleep in. I wasn't a drinker, so the cup of tea, with extra sugar, was comforting as I looked out the window.

I sent eight more texts to Emily, as if talking to an old friend.

I tried calling her, but she didn't answer. She did respond with an 'Ok' to another text.

I told her we were held up and we would be there soon.

Another text told her that I wanted to help her, take her with us and do what we could for her family. Even mentioning that if my family was the same, we would do it together.

I sat for a while after sending all those texts, wondering if I was bothering her.

Finally, I got a lengthy reply.

'This is so hard, so painful,' she wrote. 'My babies are crying, my husband is crying. I can't do anything to make it better. I have to feed them and take them to the bathroom. Nothing I do is comforting.'

'I know.' I replied. 'I can't even imagine.'

'I hope you never have too. Goodnight.'

'Goodnight. See you soon.'

And then she replied oddly.

'See.' With a laughing emoji.

I stared at that for a while, then again, attempted my husband and kids.

After burying myself in the phone and tea, I finally placed down my phone on the small table in my room. I grabbed a cracker from the snack plate I brought with me and walked to the window and opened the blinds.

When I opened them, it was breathtaking.

I faced the famed strip of Las Vegas.

It was lit up, as if nothing was happening.

A beam of light from the pyramid shaped hotel shot to the sky.

I felt as if something was missing from it all, that I was being deceived. From my vantage point, the Las Vegas strip looked like life.

No smoke, no flames, things I swore were there before. In my mind I imagined gamblers and tourists, walking the strip, unaware of the fate of the world. As if sheltered by something.

A knock on my door drew my attention and I muttered out, "Come in."

The door opened and Trace walked in.

"I'm not bothering you, am I?" he asked.

"No. Just staring out. Drinking my tea. Nibbling on these weird crackers."

He stepped inside and paused as he walked to me. I saw him staring down at my phone on the table. "Anything?"

"From my family? No."

"I'm sorry."

I sadly nodded and took a sip of my tea.

"Emily?" he asked.

"A few words. Not much. I told her we'd be back for her."

"And what did she say?"

"Not much. You're welcome to read the exchange."

"Nah." He walked to me. "I'll take your word on it." He looked out the window. "Wow."

"I know, right."

"It looks as if nothing happened there."

"I was thinking the same thing. Bright lights. No fires. Maybe it was spared."

"It wasn't." he pulled up a chair. "But it's good to look at."

"I wish I got to see it, but that wish is nothing compared to wishing my family is all right."

"It won't be long."

"So …" I faced him. "What brings you here?"

"Will and Wren are sleeping. I heard you in here. I'm checking on you. Making sure you're okay."

"I'm doing as best as I can."

"That's good."

"You?"

Trace produced a closed mouth smile then said, "I am fortunate. I have my son."

"What about your wife?"

"She died a long time ago. Thankfully, long before the problems with Will started."

"I'm sorry you went through that. You alluded to it on the plane."

"It was a difficult time," Trace said. "Definitely comes with some PTSD."

"I bet."

"But she passed," Trace placed his hand on the edge of the window. "She took her own life."

"Trace, I am sorry."

He shook his head. "I am just glad she didn't have to see any of this."

"Trace?"

"Yeah."

"Are you religious?" I asked.

"No. Why?"

"Neither am I, but hearing Mallory and Wren talk. And then she said about that religious station."

"Are you worried this is God's end?" he asked.

"I am."

"Shelb, one of them spoke of the bible and the other a television show. This isn't God's end. I can almost guarantee it. Find a bible, I am sure we can read through and dismiss it."

I brought my tea to my lips. "I don't need the bible." I looked out again. "A part of it's comforting to think it's God's end. This part of it is infuriating. Like, how can he do this to people? Maybe we interpreted it all wrong."

"I don't know."

"Do you believe in God?" I asked.

"No," he answered without hesitation. "I never did. I'm a man of science so there's no way to me that it's God's end. But if there is a God and he shows me otherwise, I'll bite."

That made me chuckle. "You'll bite."

"I take it you believe?" he asked.

"I do. And it's funny. You spend your life believing. I spent my life believing my prayers were heard and listened to. But now, with all this happening, I don't want to believe."

"There is another explanation to what's happening. We just have to find it."

I hoped he was right.

"We'll get to your family."

Just when he said that my phone rang.

Without seeing who was calling, I immediately filled with hope that it was my husband. I ran to retrieve it, but the number wasn't home. It was Emily.

"Hello," I answered rushed. "Emily?""

"Shelb."

"I'm here. How are you?" I asked. "First thing in the morning we will be there. I promise."

"I know," she said, then followed with a sob. "I hope you don't have to face this."

"We'll face it together. I'll be there soon," I said.

"Thank you. But this is too hard. I can't watch this. I can't watch my family go through this."

"Emily, listen, I know it's hard. But tomorrow, we'll be there to help."

"Shelb?" her voice cracked. "I'm sorry."

"What do you mean? What are you sorry for?"

"I can't," she said. "I just can't."

And the line went dead.

CHAPTER SIXTEEN – THE NEXT DAY

I woke up to reality. Rather, to a bad reality. That feeling that all is fine quickly turned to, 'I am not in a place I need to be. I'm not home. I'm not with my family.'

Closing my eyes I tried to take in the bad feeling, to process it, but nothing was working.

How many people had died?

The world was not the same.

How badly things had changed in the blink of an eye.

I was certain nothing additional happened, at least that I knew of, while I slept. But I could tell by looking out the window that everything was worse. I fell asleep peacefully the night before, barely dreaming and when I did, I didn't remember what exactly I dreamt. I just know that whatever it was, I forgot the world ended and when I opened my eyes the grayness of my room, even at seven o'clock in the morning, told me a lot.

It didn't feel right. Everything was off.

I got up and immediately walked to that window. Like a kid hoping for a snow day, I had a feeling. Only it wasn't excitement, it was dread. It wasn't one I was wishing for.

Having lived most of my life in Ohio, mainly Cleveland, I knew what that gloomy feeling of the day was like. The familiar hue it cast over a room, the sounds of pattering as the rain hit against the window.

A few cracks of thunder.

That was Ohio.

But we were in Las Vegas. How could this be?

The day before the skies were sunny and clear, the weather was hot. Unbearably, hot. And when I looked out the window, everything had changed. I knew from experience that the rain was cold. It was causing steam as it hit the hot ground. An ominous low cloud hovered over Las Vegas.

Had the city even seen fog before?

The rain was steady.

And it didn't look like it was stopping.

That view of the famous Las Vegas strip was for lack of a better word gloomy.

Gray and desolate. Not like the night before. It was dark, no lights.

I had to turn from the window.

The first thing I did was check my phone. No calls from my family or Emily. I tried calling her and when she didn't answer, I sent her a text saying it wouldn't be long and to hang on.

Then I called my family.

Again, no answer.

Knowing I had to find the others, I washed quickly and got dressed, really not knowing where I was going or where everyone else was.

I never bothered to see where they were sleeping or make plans to find them in the morning.

As I started to venture out, I was grateful that I saw Will walking in the hallway.

He was headed my way and I walked to him.

"I was just coming to find you," he said. "Our ride leaves in twenty minutes."

"Our ride?" I asked.

"Back to the car. Come and get some coffee."

"Thank you."

Not that I was thinking about coffee, I was thinking more about leaving. But I was hungry.

In such a gentlemanly fashion he took my backpacks "Let's

get you some food," he said. "Before we head out. Dad and Wren are there in the food hall now."

"Have you talked to Wren? Can he fly in this weather?"

"He said he would fly."

I felt a sense of relief. Then I remembered Emily and I pulled out my phone to see if she replied.

She hadn't.

"Everything alright?" he asked. "I mean it's not, but is anything different?"

I handed him my phone with the Emily message exchange open. "I'm worried. What do you make of it?"

Will paused in walking and read the exchange. "I can see why you're worried. But I think she's just grieving for what her family is going through." He handed me back my phone. "She'll feel better when we're back and she has our support."

"I hope. It just … her message sounded so final."

"Do you think she may have done something?"

"That crossed my mind."

Assuredly Will shook his head. "Having been there. Although not in this situation, but down you know, that text is a cry for help, not a cry of goodbye."

I clutched my phone and pursed my lips. "Let's hope"

Everything felt so desperate. Like that feeling of missing a good deal or trying to finish something before a deadline. An internal feeling or rush that could only be accomplished by moving forward but stuck in a sludge.

But how would I get out of that emotional quicksand? Moving forward to what? It was more like just moving. That the day wasn't going to bring any better news than the previous one.

Will and I arrived at the food hall. Will pointed me in the direction of the food line where I got coffee and eggs then joined the table with Wren and Trace.

The eggs were good, they only needed a little salt.

"How'd you sleep?" Wren asked.

"Okay," I told him. "I'm anxious to get home and to check in on Emily beforehand."

"Us, too." Wren said.

"Will told me you can fly in this weather."

Wren nodded. "It's Vegas. It will stop soon and the skies will get blue."

"What if it doesn't?" I asked.

"As long as there are no electrical storms we can move forward."

He spoke with confidence, and the man did fly the president in Air Force One. Only the best pilots did that. So, I absorbed his confidence.

"The only challenge we face," Wren said. "Is between here and the plane we get."

I knew what he alluded to and knew that more than flying back East our biggest task would be to get back to the airport. Across a broken city with death all around. Before even getting on that plane, we needed to get Emily and her family.

Going straight to the airport would be the easiest thing to do, skipping Emily, with no stops or no picking them up.

It wouldn't be the humanitarian thing to do.

With all that was happening in the world, which wasn't an option. We needed to hold onto our humanity. Anything less wasn't an option.

Mallory greeted us before we left.

"Make sure those of you who can and want to, please come back," Mallory said. "We can't move forward if we don't have the people to do so. It's still early, we need to plan for the future, whatever that holds."

She was right. We did need to plan, not to just survive, but to live in a future with those who couldn't hear or see or both. Everyone had to be taught again so they didn't rely on someone to eat or live.

"Are you open to the public? I know that sounds strange," said Will. "But if we run across anyone, can we send them here?"

"Yes," Mallory replied. "Yes. You can. We're not going

anywhere."

I once heard a saying that you cannot take care of others unless you take care of yourself. It sounded selfish, putting one's self first, but I had to take care of my family. That was what was important to me first, before I did anything else I had to get to my family.

Taking care of them, finding out about them, was taking care of myself.

I just wanted to get on that plane and get back home. Find out if they were okay. I prayed that they were. I also prayed that Emily was all right. Something felt off. That last conversation she and I shared. Now after trying, I heard nothing from her. We were twenty minutes away. It wouldn't be long.

We finished up our breakfast and conversation with Mallory. Trace and Wren both said they would probably come back after they help me. Maybe I would bring my family with me. Mallory said that would be fine, being around others was best. I wasn't certain I could do it alone if my family was like Emily's.

That was my main concern. The now and what happened in literally a flash. I knew Mallory had mentioned the seismic activity, but I didn't think it affected us. That was just a coincidence perhaps. I mean, really, how bad could the earthquakes be?

The rain did slow down, but the skies didn't clear. It was strangely muggy. But it was weather I was used to. We were given a ride to where we left the car or close to it as they could get us. It was a short walk.

We found the car where we left it the day before. No one blocked us in. It was only a few minutes from Emily's. I sent her a text.

Of course, no reply.

Taking the same route, we took to Nellis, we made our way back to Emily's home.

We kept our promise.

"Emily said she was getting an MRI, right?" Trace asked.

I nodded. "Yeah, she was at a center not far from the

municipal building. Why?"

"I wonder if she would let me examine her husband or children," Trace replied. "I mean it would be helpful if we could look, see medically if something is happening and if we can help. I can look at their eyes and into their ears, but doing an MRI would be amazing."

My first inclination was to say that we didn't have time, that I wanted to get home. Then after a few seconds of thinking about it, Trace finding anything out would benefit my family if I were faced with them losing their sight and hearing.

"Could you see that?" I asked.

"Yes, I definitely could see if there was damage to the frontal lobe or occipital lobe. I'm sure it would show. It had to."

"Now, my questions," said Wren. "They have doctors of radiology who understand that and techs to run the machines. What about that?"

Before he could answer, Will laughed. "Twenty years my dad was the doctor, the tech and the radiologist in a small town in Montana. He did all the testing. Surprised he didn't do the bloodwork as well."

"I did, when Nancy wasn't around," Trace said. "I was a small-town doctor. Some rich rancher with back issues built our MRI center. It was crazy and I learned to read them well. Actually, people from other small towns came to us."

"How did you end up in Cleveland?" I asked.

Trace pointed to Will. "Long story and that started my long story as well. Something we can share when we have down time."

"I think it's a good idea," I said. "I mean, I want to get home, but if we're armed with a way to help people, I want to carry that home with me."

"We have a lot of daylight flight time left," said Wren. "And I love flying at night too. I don't have a problem. I say we do it."

Will added. "I'm sure Emily won't mind at all."

"If she does," I said, my attention drawn to looking out the window. "We can just grab one of them."

It came from my mouth before I realized what I was saying. Narrating in real time what I witnessed as we drove near to Emily's home.

Emily lived only a few blocks from a busy portion of town.

Six or so blocks from the municipal building.

When we were there the day before, the streets were barren. No one was around.

Now that had changed.

There were people. There was movement and it was sad.

I suppose those people affected woke up unable to see or hear. They probably were in a panicked state at first, who wouldn't be.

Feeling their way around darkness, in a total state of shock and maybe denial.

The basic human instinct to survive kicked in.

Their brain still had coherent thoughts even if they couldn't express them. They probably knew if they didn't do something, they would die.

I supposed my first inkling, had it been me, would be bumping into someone else. Another human. That would have told me I was not alone.

Had it been me, what would I do?

Cry at first, scream out even if I didn't hear my own voice. Then I would vividly try to remember where I was. Feeling my way around.

It was hard to comprehend or to even imagine what they were going through.

Basic human needs, water, food, the bathroom was like being through into a pitch blank room with ear plugs in.

As if fate said, 'Find your way. Good luck.'

But the will to survive was strong.

If I could help them I would, but I needed to get to Emily, to my family.

It was a weak inner promise, but I made one to myself, that when we got Emily and her family and found a testing area so Trace could examine them, I would do something for anyone we saw.

Get them water, food, a miniscule gesture in the scope of things, but it would help them.

"So many now," said Will. "Where were they yesterday?"

"Recovering emotionally," Trace said. "They grieved what they lost and then realized they had to live."

"This can't be the whole world, right?" Will asked. "It can't be the new normal."

We turned the bend from the main road to a residential street. Those people walking began fading from our view.

"Image," Trace spoke softly. "These people, at least half of them will learn to function and function well. When a sense is lost, another takes over. They'll find that and embrace it. If they live long enough."

"That's what Mallory is talking about," said Wren. "If we help them now. Help them learn, they won't need us."

"Or maybe this is all temporary," said Trace. "It could be. I mean, the body could heal itself. What if tomorrow or the next day, or even a couple months, everything comes back to them."

"Could it?" asked Will.

"Yes. It could."

"I shudder to think," I added. "What will happen to the world in the meantime?"

Unlike the busier portion or commercial roads, the quiet street had no wandering people.

"First and foremost," Trace stated as the car slowed down. "We talk to Emily."

I glanced out the window as we pulled up to Emily's house.

My stomach felt my heart plunge down to it.

The blinds were closed, the front door shut. I just had a sickening feeling.

"Something isn't right," I said. "Something is wrong. My gut is telling me something is wrong."

Trace sighed out heavily. "I hear you. We can't base that on that text message you got. But there's only one way to find out."

"It's early," Will said. "They're probably sleeping."

Everyone opened their doors at the same time. Wren, Trace, and Will.

I didn't.

I was scared to get out.

I just knew. I knew by looking at the house, replaying my last conversation with Emily, that everything was wrong.

I didn't need to be a psychic to know what Emily did.

The question was, did I want to see it?

No.

After the three of them walked to the front door, I finally got out.

Trace looked back at me. "Are you coming?"

"I'll wait here."

And I did. Standing in the middle of the walkway, a good distance from the house.

It was dark, dismal and foretelling. They had to see it. Feel it.

There was a slight tremble to my hands that radiated through my body. A nervousness laced with a feeling of doom.

Trace knocked on the door and rang the bell.

After a few moments, and no answer, he looked over his shoulder at Wren.

Wren nodded.

Trace tried the knob and opened the door.

That was when I saw it.

The flinch.

Trace flinched.

I watched him step back, turn his head and cover his mouth. He looked at the others, said something I couldn't hear and then went inside.

That was all I needed to see.

His reaction told me there was a smell and a bad one at that.

All three of them walked inside and I turned my back to the house.

Arms folded tight to my body I listened for sounds, for voices, but it was only silence.

How long did I stand there, not looking at the house, staring at the ground?

I jumped a little when I felt a hand on my shoulder. Turning slightly, Wren stood there.

"They're dead, aren't they?" I asked.

Wren nodded. "You were right. Something was wrong. She killed them. The husband. The two kids. Drowned the ..."

"I don't want to know." I closed my eyes tight. A gut-wrenching burn swept over my body. Was it pain, anger, sadness?

Her children were so young, they probably didn't even know what was happening.

Why I would do it to myself, I didn't know. It was sadistic. I kept trying to imagine what someone felt after suddenly losing sight and hearing, I couldn't' imagine the horror of being in that silent darkness and plunged into death.

What her husband felt. Her children felt. Trusting her. Feeling her soft reassuring touch then suddenly unable to breathe.

It was time to go. I just wanted to leave.

"Shelb," Trace softly called my name. "What do we do?"

I thought perhaps he meant about the bodies. Did we take time to bury them or leave them like so many other bodies that would just rot away in the heat?

What should we do?

"I don't know," I replied.

"Shelb. I need to know."

"Why are you asking me?" I snapped.

"Because you're a mom. What would you want us to do?"

That question puzzled me and when I turned around to ask him what he meant, I got my answer.

He wanted to know what we should do. Not about the kids, not about the husband, but Emily.

What we should do with Emily.

She stood with Trace looking in shock, despondent, but unlike her family, she was very much alive.

CHAPTER SEVENTEEN - THE AIRPORT

She killed her children.
I don't know how, I didn't listen to how.
She killed her husband.

It was a strange moment. I didn't know how to react. A part of me felt I should hate what she did, be angry for how she didn't give her family a choice.

I was numb.

I wanted to embrace her because I could see on her face the pain she felt. She was grieving whether she brough it upon herself or not, she was hurting.

Her family was dead and, in a part, I think to her, they were dead before she killed them.

I was torn in what or how I should feel.

It wasn't for me to judge her. I kept telling myself that, yet there I was judging her. My role in all this was nothing. I was neither a leader nor follower. I was just a mother wanting to get home.

Perhaps I would understand her decision in due time.

It was easy to imagine being the strong supportive mother helping her family in need. But what if the family in need was suffering more than help was available?

A small child suddenly unable to hear or see, thrust into darkness and silence.

Maybe that was all I saw, the loss of hearing and sight. Maybe there was more to the suffering, a pain maybe.

Whatever the case, Emily took the lives of her family not in some selfish move but in some sort of chivalrous move to save them. Or was it?

I had to keep telling myself that. The mother in me wanted to be angry. I fought that.

Emily got in the car, said nothing, stared outward and asked no question.

Where were we going?

Was it the airport?

I kept thinking about Trace's plan to do testing on her family. How that went out the window. While there were so many affected, who were blind and deaf, we could grab and test, there was something unscrupulous about just snatching someone off the street and throwing them into an MRI.

They wouldn't know what was happening or understand. It wasn't easy to explain.

Surely, someone out there other than Trace was wanting to test those who lost senses due to the event.

When exactly did the event end up being low on the totem pole of things to find out?

I was more interested in if the blind could be cured more than why they were blind.

Our goal now was to get to the airport and have Wren find a plane that would work.

One we could fuel up and prepare to fly east.

I sat in the back seat with Emily, and honestly, I didn't talk to her, mainly because I didn't know what to say.

She just looked out the window then forward.

I thought of my children, my husband, and getting home.

During the ride, I looked out the window. None of us mentioned that so many people wandered aimlessly. I felt horrible not helping them or doing something. I kept telling myself that if they made it to the street, they were making progress.

Focusing on surviving.

Like I was.

Perhaps that was my way of justifying why I didn't call out, stop the car.

After I found my family, I could look at helping others.

It wouldn't be fair to those I loved if I delayed my trip home to help those I didn't know.

Plus, no one in the car bothered calling out and suggesting we help.

We arrived at the airport and it wasn't like a normal thing. Wren drove to the tarmac and parked the car.

He said he would need to check for a plane, check the fuel and then we could go.

Until then, we could wait outside or go in.

It was hot and muggy, maybe that was the reason I agreed to go inside. There were two or three planes he wanted to try.

He said he would find us when he was able to get me home.

I had to remind myself that Wren didn't need to do this. He didn't need to play the hero pilot and take me home. I had resolved myself to be appreciative and remember that he could have easily stayed at Nellis.

Trace took Emily's arm, being compassionate but saying very little.

Wil led the way.

Using a portable staircase, we walked up to a skybridge, then through into the terminal.

We emerged into a gate, slot machines were everywhere, tinkling and ringing.

While there were bodies on the ground, in seats, more of them moved about aimlessly.

It was cold in there, the AC blasted and without the sun beating through the windows, it was chilly.

It was a strange smell as well, everything bagels mixed with a hint of death.

As soon as we stepped into the terminal, Emily started to cry.

I didn't get it, it a part of me was irritated.

Why was she crying?

Was she scared?

It was a little too late to cry for her family.

In a strange, even for me move, I walked away and to an empty slot machine. It was odd to do and not really the time, but I had a twenty-dollar bill in my wallet and I put that in the machine.

I just wanted to be away from the crying, and I wanted to go home.

Not knowing what I was doing, I hit the spin button.

Nothing was happening, the reels would spin with no win.

In a few minutes, Will was next to me, doing the same.

"You okay?" he asked, then looked over his shoulder at his father and Emily as they sat down.

"I guess." I said. "I just want to get home."

"We'll get you there."

"Then what for you?" I asked.

"I don't know." He pressed the button on the machine. "Between you and me I'm not feeling really compelled to help her. But then a part of me wants to."

"I'm torn, too." I said.

"Why is that?"

"I mean, she did what she thought was best. I don't think it was out of anger or maliciousness."

"Me either."

"Yet, I don't know how to feel. I want to be compassionate, I know she's in pain, my God, she has to be in pain, but I want to be angry."

"Look," he said and pressed, "Oh man this suck." He said of his machine.

"Mine, too."

"We can't begin to understand why she did what she did. The world is not the same."

"No, it is not."

"Who is to say we wouldn't make the same choice?"

"Me." I faced him, stopping the play on my machine. "I could never kill my children. What? Because they can't see or hear? I love them. I love my kids. To drown them or suffocate them is horrible. They didn't know it was coming. And to do so … especially, since your dad brought up the fact that it could be temporary."

"But did she know that?" Will asked. "All she knew was her family was in a dead dark, silence."

"She still killed them." I lowered my head, pausing and closing my eyes. "I am so torn on how I should feel. She didn't know. She wanted to stop their suffering, I am guessing, because none of us asked her."

"Then do it," Will suggested. "Go ask her why she did it."

"Can I? Should I?"

"Yes." Will nodded. "Me? I don't care. The deed is done. But we may be all that's left that can walk, talk, see and hear. I know you want your family to be fine, but God forbid they aren't, we all need each other. Ask her."

Ask her.

That was a lot easier said than done. How does one just walk up to a woman and ask, "Why did you kill your children?"

After I finished playing my twenty dollars, I decided to ask her. I had the courage. She had been seated in a waiting area far from the bodies, one that was probably empty before the event. When I looked there, she wasn't anywhere.

I wondered if I should find her or tell Will. Just as I decided to look and call out for her, I noticed the people that moved aimlessly, actually went moving and feeling about aimlessly. They were by the bagel sandwich stand.

The smell of food called to them.

They were hungry and that sense kicked in.

Despite the ones we saw on the plane, these poor people needed to eat.

"Will," I called him. "Hey look." I pointed to the bagel stand.

"What?"

"They're following the scent of food." I headed that way.

"Where are you going?"

"To feed them."

"Shelb, that's not a good idea."

He blurted out something else, another warning, but I made my way there. As I was trying to sneak around one of them, his head turned.

He couldn't see me, his eyes were hazed over, and I was certain he didn't hear me. The way he lifted his head, it was like he sensed me, maybe smelled my deodorant.

I slipped by his reached out arm. His fingers grazed against my skin. It felt creepy. And after lifting the hinged counter, I made it into the back of the bagel sandwich stand.

Now what?

There were bagels and bread, lunch meat and chips. Everything I needed to make sandwiches and standing there, gathered around that sandwich stand had to be about twenty people all reaching aimlessly for food, grabbing thin air.

Once and a while, someone grabbed something edible.

How would I do it? How would I feed them? They couldn't see or hear but they could smell and they knew they needed food.

I thought back to when Trace was teaching Emily how to tell her husband about water. How he touched his palm, making the letter W before placing a bottle in his hand.

I found a knife and cut a bagel, first in half then in fours. I knew it wasn't much, but it was a small enough start.

Before handing any of them out, I put at least a dozen bottles of water on the counter. Maybe they would find them while reaching. The food wasn't as easy.

I was nervous.

With a small piece of bagel in my hand I looked at the reaching and wandering people, finding the easiest one to approach. One that didn't scare me or seem desperate.

It was a woman, an older woman.

She looked harmless and as scared as I felt.

I took a piece of bagel and walked to her from behind the counter.

She lifted her head as if smelling and I reached for her hand. She immediately withdrew it, as if scared from my touch and I grabbed her hand again, this time, placing the piece of bagel in it. I closed her fingers around it and brought her hand to her nose.

She smiled when she smelled it and immediately started to eat it.

One down.

I could get her water, but I wanted to try another person with food. I went back to the counter, prepared more and carried a basket with me.

Making my way back from that counter, I approached another person, doing the same thing. That was successful, but then as I tried to distribute more something happened. It was as if they sensed someone was giving them food and they began to grow anxious, pushing forward to me aggressively, arms out, grabbing, swinging.

They didn't mean to be hostile, I didn't think so, but they reached and desperately tried.

Hating to do so, I knew I had to make my escape and that was when I was struck.

Someone reaching, swinging aimlessly, clocked me in the side of the face just below my left eye and I saw stars.

My legs began to buckle at the shock of being hit and my balance went off. I tried not to go down, but I lost my footing and I did.

Never in my life had I experienced anything as surreal and frightening as the moment I hit the ground, under the feet of a hungry mob. They couldn't hear me cry for help or see me.

I felt feet stomping my head, throat, chest, legs and stomach. I could barely breathe and it was taking everything I had to fight that and get up. It was a battle I was losing.

I was just there, on the ground, trying to get out. They weren't moving forward, they were moving in circles and just pouncing on me.

This was it.

With my ability to breathe decreasing, my body aching from the constant thumps, I was ready to succumb. My consciousness was fading. I was going in and out of awareness, the pain stopped and I felt as if I were floating.

No longer was breathing an issue. I felt fine, euphoric. Why?

I was dying.

Helpless to do anything but surrender to the situation.

Then I felt a hand grab on to my arm and I was pulled up.

What exactly was happening, who had me and how I got out of there was blurry.

All I knew was one moment I was being stomped, suffocated and killed, the next I could breathe.

There was a blackout period. I was in that desperate situation then I was in a chair and being handed water by Trace.

"Take a breath," he said, placing his ear to my chest. "Okay some lung sounds." He stood up and looked at me. "Shelb, look at me. Let me see your eyes."

He was out of focus.

"Okay listen. You've been injured. I need to know where it hurts."

"Everywhere," I replied.

I wanted to talk to him, to focus, but it was hard. Like looking through water. Everything was blurry and distorted.

Trace spoke to Will and even Emily was there. They were saying things to each other and I didn't know what was being said.

Muffled words of fear, back and forth. Sentences that sounded foreign to me.

The pain from my chest, side and throat throbbed with each beat of my heart making it impossible to know what they were saying.

"Rest," said Trace. "We have you."

Rest. Okay. That sounded easy enough. My body had been through an unbelievable trauma. Beaten, stomped, and discarded. Like a crowd rushing to a concert stage and I was caught in the wave of a stampede.

I closed my eyes. Not just because I wanted to, but because I didn't have a choice. My eyes were heavy, I was depleted.

I didn't have time to think about what had happened. Why I put myself in that position. How it went from me trying to feed desperate people affected by the event to me in danger.

I was depleted. My body was in pain and my ability to stay awake was difficult.

When my eyes closed, I thought I would sleep or pass out. Instead, I slipped into a state where I was aware of what was going on but unable to make my body do anything. I couldn't talk or move.

Was this death?

Did I fall victim to the event?

All of it crossed my mind. A freight train of thoughts cruised through my mind in an aware darkness. I felt the movement but couldn't see.

I was at the mercy of those around me.

For a brief moment, with all the pain, I just wished I would die. Then I thought I did.

Everything went black.

CHAPTER EIGHTEEN – THE NEXT FLIGHT

I don't know how long I was out, or at least I didn't when I woke up. But I woke up grateful that I could hear. The sound of rushing air, like a white noise in overdrive, caused me to open my eyes.

I could see.

I was laying down on some extended bed seat, a blanket covered me and I had a pillow. As soon as I tried to move a pain shot through my side.

"Easy, easy." Trace said.

"I didn't die?"

"No. You passed out. We brought you on the plane."

Again, I struggled to sit up and Trace helped me. Glancing around, I realized I was on a different type of plane, the seats were separated and instead of one window I had three.

"What kind of plane is this?" I asked.

"First class on a plane used for international flights. That's what Wren found. I'm not complaining, are you?"

"For the seats, no. The pain, did I break something?"

"I think a rib or two, it's hard to tell. Binding is a thing of the past, but I think we should bind you when we can. I only found ibuprofen for the pain. But know how badly a broken rib feels, I would opt for the medicinal marijuana gummies Will found or booze."

"I'll get that for you. Stay still."

"Anything else?" I asked.

"You passed out hard and fortunately," Trace said. "They had a pretty decent first aid kit on the plane. I bandaged that cheek even though I think it needs a stich or two."

"Are we on our way to Cleveland?"

"We are," Trace answered.

"How long was I out?"

"Thirty minutes. We're in the air. Let me mix you something up for pain and I'll be right back."

"Thank you."

The moment Trace left Will appeared.

"Hey," he said.

"Hey."

"Have you ever seen first class like this?" he asked.

"I've only seen first class when I walked through it to the back of the plane."

"Me, too. But this is nice. There's food. Wren found it in a refrigeration unit. It's warming now. So cool."

"Little trays."

"Yep." Will took a breath and exhaled. "So, like you're either the bravest person I know or the stupidest."

"Will, what happened?" I asked.

"I'm not sure. I was telling you not to feed them, but you did and they mobbed you. Not like the eight passengers on our flight, but like a concert."

"That's the feeling I felt, like they were rushing the stage."

"I saw you and then you were gone."

"Who pulled me out?" I asked.

"I did."

"Thank you."

"Shelby, it's a different world now. I know you think we need to do our part."

"We do," I said. "We do."

"At what cost? Another minute and we wouldn't be flying you home to find your family." Will stood when Trace returned.

"Here." Trace handed me a bottle of water, a glass with

brown liquid, and a napkin with four pills. "Sip this and take these."

"Excuse me." Will stood. "I'm going to go see how Wren is doing and if he needs anything."

I nodded them looked at Trace, taking the pills, placing them in my mouth, then washing them down with the water. I then grabbed the glass. "Thank you."

"It won't take away all the pain, but once we pass a pharmacy, I'll find you something. Like I said I want to bind those ribs. You're a lucky woman. You were trampled."

"And I remember each and every step." I sipped the liquid. And with each sip I was hoping the pain would stop. It wasn't just the sharp unbearable pain in my chest, my head hurt and my face hurt. Everything hurt. "What is this?"

"Brandy."

"Just relax and enjoy the view. I'd say enjoy a movie, but it seems the internet is down now."

"Any more radio contact?" I asked.

"You know what? Let me check." He tapped me on my leg like a doctor making a house call and stepped away.

Then came Emily.

I honestly thought we lost her. I hadn't seen her, at least I didn't see her when I went to the bagel stand.

She sat down in the row across from me and the way that the first class was set up, she was slightly a row ahead. In her seat she stared forward, saying nothing, then she turned in her chair.

"When I was first married, I broke a rib, fake wrestling with my husband, fooling around, you know." She sighed. "It hurt for weeks. I'm sorry. I know the pain."

I didn't say anything, I sipped the drink.

"I'm sorry this happened to you."

Again, a nod and a sip and then it slipped out. I wasn't even thinking, the words were out of my mouth before I could do anything. "Why did you do it?"

She lowered her head. "I was waiting for that from you."

"No one else asked?"

Emily shook her head.

"I'm going to be honest with you. A part of me feels it's not my place to judge you and another part of me is angry."

"I don't blame you, because I'm angry," she said. "I'm angry at what I did. I'm angry at what happened to my family and I'm angry because I couldn't do it to myself. I want to die Shelby. My kids are dead. I don't want to live."

"Why did you do it?"

"Because I felt desperation," she replied. "My kids couldn't go to the bathroom, didn't understand how to eat. Their sight and hearing were gone. They weren't born into a world of darkness and silence, they were thrust into it. They didn't understand what was happening and couldn't speak to express how they felt. I was trying. I suppose not very hard and not for very long. Trying to feed them was so hard. I knew, or felt, they'd be better off not living. I sunk. I had sunk into some dark place and in my mind, I truly felt death was the answer. Am I sorry? Oh my God, I hate myself. I do want to die. I tried, but I was a coward."

"I can't judge you," I said. "I can only listen to what you are saying."

"And I am not looking for forgiveness or understanding. I don't expect it."

"I know as a mother, I love my children beyond life."

"And you feel you'd never do that?"

I nodded.

"I would say the same thing. Until I was faced with how my children and husband were and how they'd survive."

"They weren't dead, they were sick."

"I know. I made that choice," she said. "I made that choice in a moment of desperation and regret it with everything I am. As I said, I want to die now, right now. But a part of me wants to live so I can feel the pain that I caused myself."

I didn't know what to say to her. I heard her words, what she said, and I didn't know how I would feel if faced with the same choice. My children were also older than hers.

Emily's children were young, they relied on help to survive.

There was silence between us for a moment. After silence in Emily's confession and me thinking about what she said.

During that moment, Trace, Will and Wren came into first class.

"We took the plane," Wren said. "I took it. Obviously, someone is watching. I just got a radio call asking us to identify ourselves. It's not a bad thing, someone out there watching the sky tells me life is still going on. I bring this up because I didn't reply. I will. What do you want me to say if they tell us to land? Should we land or continue to Cleveland."

He looked at me for an answer. "Do what your gut tells you."

Wren gave me a single nod and turned, walking back to the cockpit.

"What does that mean?" Trace asked.

"He got us in the sky, he is taking me home. If he lands, he lands because he's fearful if we don't. Either way, someone calling out to him is a good sign."

As hard as it physically was, with Trace's assistance, I made my way to the cockpit. The hard part was getting out of the seat. Once I was up, it didn't hurt nearly as much as when seated and changing positions. Because of that, I decided to stand.

"Anything?" I asked Wren.

"Just talking to them now," Wren replied, then with a couple push of knobs, I could hear the person on the other end of the radio."

"And you don't have a flight number?" asked the person.

"Are you really looking for a flight number? Right now, with all that's going on?" Wren retorted. "Look as I said before I am a pilot. We were stranded in Las Vegas after whatever event that was and I prepped a plane to leave."

"We? How many of you are on the plane now?" the man on the radio asked.

"Five. Who am I speaking to?"

"This is Sergeant Naples, air control at Colorado Springs

Space Force. And you?"

"Captain Wren Lockhart."

"Senior Pilot Air Force One," said Naples.

"That's correct."

"Wow, I whispered. You're famous in the sky."

Wren gave a crocked smile.

Naples continued, "We've been monitoring the skies and you are the first plane we've seen since everything went down yesterday."

"Went down, literally you mean?" Wren asked.

"Almost every plane in the sky. Were you on the ground?"

"No, in the air."

There I was listening. They were conversing as if it were a normal conversation between two friends.

"You obviously weren't the pilot on the plane you were on at the time of the event," said Naples.

"I wasn't. How did you know?"

"Other than you told me who you were, your eyes had to be covered by at least an inch and ears blocked into the canal, like ear buds. The pilot flying the plane would not have that."

"So, you guys know for a fact that's what prevented us from being infected."

"Yes or not exposed to sunlight or the noise. Like a sound booth or underground."

"We were fortunate that the flight deck was open or we would have gone down," said Wren.

"Where are you headed."

"Cleveland international."

There was a pause, a long pause, and it seemed awkward not to mention suspicious. It was long enough that Wren acknowledged my presence.

"How are you feeling?" he asked.

"Sore but alive. Why did he stop talking?"

"I don't know. Seems strange."

Naples came back on with a hiss of static before he spoke, "Cleveland, are there any plans to fly elsewhere after Cleveland?"

"Not sure," Wren answered. "We did discuss going back to Nellis. Why?"

"We need pilots. We have survivors out there. We're trying to help those who are affected and we can't get to them all. Things are happening on the ground, Captain."

"What things?"

"Falling apart, and it's not just people. Nature is kind of going nuts. We need to get the vulnerable to safety if we can."

"That's pretty humanitarian of you."

"President's orders," said Naples.

"The president is still alive?"

"He was in a safe place when it happened. So, can you? Can we count on you Captain?"

"I'll have to get back to you. I need to get a passenger to Cleveland for her family. After that, I'll make contact. Is there any way other than the radio?"

"Right now, cell towers are still operational. We expect they'll be down along with essential services in three days. Let me get you a number."

It felt strange, like eavesdropping on a telephone call, only they were on the radio. All standard radio procedures were out the window, they didn't do the overs and outs.

Wren offered me to sit in the other front seat, I declined because it felt better to stand. I listened to him make arrangements to help out after he helped me.

I realized how lucky I was that I was on the flight with him, when everything happened. That not only did he save us by landing the plane, but he was also going to get me home then move on to help others. I also realized I knew nothing other than he was a pilot on suspension.

That needed to change. I owed him that much to ask about his life, if of course, he wanted to share. After all, we were surviving strangers, but strangers with a rare bond. We could still see and hear, unlike most of the survivors out there.

CHAPTER NINETEEN – FRIENDLY SKIES

It was just after I started my 'who is Wren' conversation, that Trace and Will both made their way to the flight deck to find out what was going on. Emily didn't. She stayed in her seat.

I did get some information from him. At thirty-eight years old Wren was accomplished. He dedicated his life to his country. He wasn't married, came close once. No children. His life was his career. It seemed inconceivable to me that one drink in a hotel room could derail his career. But he wasn't bitter, he wasn't angry, he just accepted the fact.

"I for one am glad you were suspended," Will said. "If you hadn't been. You wouldn't have been on this plane and we would be toast."

"Not really," said Wren. "If I recall you were looking up how to land a plane."

"I have a question," I said. "That guy on the radio, said the president was in a safe place. As someone that knew and worked with the president, how did he know to get in a safe place if no one knew the event was coming?"

"That's a good point," Will stated.

"Not really," Wren replied.

"Sorry," I said with sarcasm. "It's just an observation."

"No. no, I didn't mean it like that," Wren defended. "I mean, at least once a month a surprise drill occurs where we have to get the president to safety. If he's on my plane, I have to get him there. If he's on the ground, same thing. It could be a coincidence that he happened to be in a safe place when it happened. Just like it was a coincidence you were in the bathroom."

I shrugged. "Maybe. I just find it hard to believe that all this happened in a blink of an eye and freak of nature."

Will added. "Or God."

"Whatever the reason." Trace waved out his hand. "We're here because we were where fate dictated us to be," Trace said. "I feel terrible because my whole point of this trip was to go home and bury my mother. My mother will never be buried."

"Ah, dude, for real?" Wren asked. "I'm sorry about your mother. I will bring you back if you want."

"I appreciate that," said Trace.

"Did you retire from medicine? You seem too young to retire," stated Wren.

"No." Trace shook his head. "We have something in common. We both lost our jobs to the drink. Mines a little worse. I lost my license because I drank, and I still drink. I never get drunk, just have this tolerance, but that tolerance doesn't adhere to the BHL. I saw it coming, I knew it was coming, I didn't care."

"Can we be clear?" Will asked. "My father didn't make medical mistakes. One out of town patient smelled it on him."

"Doesn't matter," Trace said. "I made my bed. I was so consumed with your addiction, that I didn't realize I was drinking myself into my own to ease the pain."

Wren looked over his shoulder at me. "What's your story?"

"Me?" I shrugged. "No story, really. I'm a mom of two teenagers, a wife. My husband is a salesman, and I work at a discount furniture store getting high interest loans for people with bad credit who need new furniture. And no disrespect to you three, but I only recently started drinking since the event."

"Sounds like me," Emily's voice entered. She spoke softly, standing in the doorway, leaning with arms crossed against her waist. "I'm sorry. I didn't mean to intrude."

"No," I told her. "It's fine. Talk to us."

"My life, except my kids are little. My husband worked in sales, but locally and I worked at the casino. Front desk."

"Dude," Will said. "That sounds like a crazy job."

"It was. I never drank though. Maybe once in a while at a social event. I want to get drunk."

"Well talk to my dad." Will nodded his head at Trace. "He's the gatekeeper of it all."

Wren laughed.

I gasped. "Will."

Trace scoffed. "it's fine. I know what I am and he knows what he is. Now's not the time to quit drinking. I have the stash from the plane. Let me know."

"I will. You all have been so kind," Emily said. "Shelb, you asked me why I killed my family. I told you I was desperate because I didn't know how they would survive."

"No one is judging you," Trace said. "If our reaction seemed like it, it's because we were shocked."

"I need to further my explanation," Emily explained. "The reason I worried about their survival is because I probably won't be here in another year. When I said I wanted to die now, I meant now. Because I will die in probably a year. Maybe sooner."

The MRI, that's what she had been doing. That was what saved her. "You were at the medical center." I said.

Emily nodded. "I have a brain tumor. A big one. They found it when I hit my head at work, then they tested more. I hadn't even told Todd, my husband yet. I was seeing what this MRI said. They wanted to operate last week. But again, I wanted another MRI before I said anything. Now … now it doesn't matter. They said more than likely, it will double in size in two months."

"Glioblastoma?" Trace asked. "Did they use that word?"

"They did."

"I'm sorry." Trace reached out to her.

My first thought was *Oh my God*. And it became super clear to me why she did what she did. Who would take care of her family if she died? The man on the radio said they were trying to help, but were there enough healthy to do so?

The thought of my mortality in the midst of my family's reliance on me, hadn't even dawned on me. Now it did. What if my husband and children were the same? How would I care for them and what would happen to them if something happened to me?

They'd be alone.

Left to fend for themselves in a cold, dark, silent world.

"I'm sorry, Emily," I told her. "I really am. The pain you have."

"I shouldn't have done it, I shouldn't have," she said. "I should have told you and asked for help. Instead, I didn't give them a choice."

"Can I tell you something," Will said. "What you did, none of us can understand. I know it has to feel horrendous, painful and a guilt that is like no other. Add that to grief. Focus on the grief right now, because it's a different world out there and none of us know what's going to happen next."

Wren nearly whispered, "Isn't that the truth."

The way he said it was alarming and when I looked back at him, I saw what he was speaking about.

"What ... is that?" Trace asked.

"I don't know," Wren replied. "It's not like any storm I have ever seen."

Storm? It looked as if we hit the end of the world. Nothing but total black was ahead of us in the distance. A big black wall blocking everything left and right, up and down.

It was just black.

"There's no lightning, nothing. What the hell is it?" Wren reached for the radio. "Colorado come in. Naples are you there."

A few seconds later, Naples replied. "We read you."

"You have anything on satellite?" Wren asked. "Massive storm, something."

"Nothing that we see. Do you have something up there."

"Yeah, we do," Wren said, "It looks like I'm staring into an abyss."

On those words he turned the plane, flying north, instead of east, moving along side of it until we determined what it was.

CHAPTER TWENTY – NOT SO FRIENDLY SKIES

The question to push forward or turn around had to be answered fast. We were running out of time. Will looked out each of the plane's front windows then he ran to the back and returned. "Oh my God. It goes all the way to the ground. We're headed north now, right? Then this thing goes north then south. I can't see around it, above it or below it. How can you?"

"I can't." Wren replied, "That's why I turned."

"But we didn't turn around," Trace said. "Are you hoping that maybe you'll come to an end of it."

Emily murdered, "Is there an end to it? Maybe this is it?"

I asked, "What would cause this?"

Wren shook his head and lifted the radio. "Colorado come in. This is Cleveland. We changed course now heading north."

"We see that," Naples said. "Did you avoid it?"

"No." Replied Wren. "We've flown about seventy-five miles and it looks like there is no end in sight heading north Are you sure you saw nothing?"

"Nothing on the weather radar. We're gonna get in touch with the space station and see what they say. I'll give them your coordinates. Hang tight."

"Roger that, should we try flying south?"

"Let me hear back from the space station."

It was odd this voice from Colorado watching us. He was a connection with the world. We didn't have. He was looking at weather satellites. We needed more of a different view. I had no idea what was happening, all I knew was that what we flew parallel to scare the hell out of me.

"Maybe we got it all wrong," Emily said. "Maybe this wasn't some terror attack. Maybe Mallory was right or rather that religious station."

"Mallory did a paraphrase of an episode of Supernatural," said Trace. "This isn't an ending made by a God. This is nature."

"Yeah," said Will. "I mean, isn't there supposed to be a rapture?"

Wren shook his head. "Different religions interpret some of the bible differently, but now."

"What if this …" Emily said. "Is the rapture. I mean the blind and deaf. All those that died. What if body and soul they didn't ascend and disappear like books depicted, what if God just took their souls."

"It's not God's end," Trace argued.

"How can you be so sure?" Emily asked.

"If I believed in God," Trace replied. "If I did, then why would I believe a God who loved his people would do this?"

I murmured, "There are no atheists in foxholes."

Almost shocked, Trace looked at me. "What? How is what I said saying I'm not an atheist."

"It wasn't. I'm just thinking. What about you Wren, you spewed forth some bible stuff with Mallory. Anything in there match this?"

Wren pursed his lips. "Uh, …' he then spoke in a reciting manner. "The sun will be darkened, the moon will not give light, the stars will fall from the sky and the heavenly bodies will be shaken."

"Whoa," said Will. "How do you just quote this shit off the top of your head?"

"My father was a minister. Simple supper conversations seemed to be a bible study more often than not …" He stopped when the radio hissed.

"Cleveland, come in," Naples said.

"We read you."

"Anyone have a cell phone, can they take a picture of what you see and send it to the number I sent you?"

"Not sure of the signal," replied Wren. "We can try."

I was on it, or at least I thought I was. I reached for my phone in my back pocket, feeling the pain in my ribs when I did. But my phone wasn't there. "My phone."

"I placed it in your bag," said Trace.

"I have mine." Will lifted the phone, went to the side window and took a picture.

Wren handed him the number.

"We're sending it," Wren said over the radio. "What did the Space station say?"

Silence.

"Naples."

The radio hissed and then over the airwaves, I heard Naples exhaled. "They see nothing."

"Well, we see something."

"No, I mean from their vantage point, it's like a black shadow over a portion of the earth. They don't know what it is," said Naples. "They're trying to communicate with a satellite that tracks people, see what's happening on the ground in that area."

"How big of an area?" Wren asked. "Can they see?"

"They say it runs from the hundredth meridian to the prime."

I shook my head not understanding. "What does that mean?"

Will actually answered. "Pretty much the great plains to somewhere in Europe."

"It'll be an hour or so," said Naples. "Until we get something to tell you. But all they see is black. That's why they want to get a closer look."

"What do we do in the meantime?" asked Wren.

"If I were you," said Naples. "I'd find a place to land and stay close to the radar. I'll help you with that if that's the course you want to take."

Wren looked at each of us as if wanting our opinion on what to do. We all gave him a look that conveyed what we thought. No words needed to be spoken. Was there even a choice? We couldn't go into a black area. A place that looked as if the powers that be dropped a black curtain over the world. We had no choice. We had to land, wherever we were.

I didn't know what that black area was, the abyss that looked like the world was cut off. I knew one thing.

My family was in that area where the anomaly had taken over and I was horrified to think what was happening there.

CHAPTER TWENTY-ONE – WHAT LIES TO THE SIDE

The hundredth meridian is an east and west divide of the United States. It runs from North Dakota to Texas, straight down the middle. It spans out some, but the black area, according to Niles, seemed to edge in somewhere around Kansas City.

We had a choice.

We could turn around and land in Denver or land in Oklahoma City, which was really close, or at least it seemed it, to the abyss.

I thought it was a matter of trust when Wren opted for Oklahoma City, telling us that once whatever it was left, it would be faster to get home.

The reason, in my mind, was to avoid being too close to Colorado.

I would.

I mean, this guy on the radio was awfully helpful.

Too helpful.

Maybe it was an enemy attack and the friendly voice in the sky was a trick to lure us back.

Either way, Wren's mind was made up.

We were landing. The skies were still blue where we headed. Seeing the difference reminded me of all those space movies and photos I saw where the sky met the black of space just above the atmosphere.

Only there were no stars in the sky.

And while we flew, there was no word from Colorado.

We took advantage of the food that we heated on the plane, the first-class meals with a choice of chicken or beef. We all ate in that hour we waited to land.

Trace collected all the bottles of booze on the plane. Not just what he could carry, but all.

Then again, why would he stop drinking now? The world was seemingly over, and salvaging as much booze as he could was his medicine.

The tiny bottle would be carried on him like I would carry water.

Addiction wasn't something I was ever faced with and knew nothing about it. I was ignorant of it. The longer I was in the air, the more I realized, I had a pretty much a perfect life.

My kids weren't always the best behaved. My husband was jealous and controlling at times. Or he tried to be controlling. It never worked, I was too head strong, and I took his jealousy those few times as a compliment.

Some wouldn't.

I did.

Money was never what I wanted, but I was happy with my children.

It was never so bad I wanted out.

It was never so bad I buried myself in drugs or alcohol.

What happened in Trace and Will's life? I always read that addiction is hereditary.

But at that moment, most of the world dead or without sight and hearing, it wasn't the time to think or judge.

I wanted to go home.

And that black thing that blocked the world was blocking my way home.

Admittedly, the more wine I sipped, the less my ribs hurt, which was the main source of my dismay and pain.

In the hour before we landed, we talked about everything but what was happening outside. I told of my beautiful teenage daughter, Layla, and how she was the captain on the cheerleading squad and had a scholarship. I showed her picture when I fetched my phone. And she did so much volunteer work. My son, Alex, not so much. He played video games and made animations.

Emily spoke of her family as if they were still alive, like none of what happened had happened to them.

I was fine with that. I, too, would do whatever it took to cope.

Wren talked about his minister father and submissive mother. How he hoped they were both alive out there, but he'd have to fly to Hawaii to search for them.

Will offered to join him, and both he and Trace talked about how it had been just them two, no one else since his mother died.

He referred to his mother dying and I wondered if he ever knew she took her own life.

A part of me was envious of those who had passed.

They didn't have to live to see the horror, wait in anticipation to find out if those they loved were alive or scalded by the event.

It felt rough as we approached our landing. The plane shook as if we were hitting turbulence.

I could feel every shake and bump. Each jolt caused a stabbing pain to my chest and side.

Wren said something over the speaker, but I couldn't hear him. Emily and Will stayed in the cabin with me, while Trace was up front.

I closed my eyes, I didn't want to see their faces in case their expressions showed the same terror I felt.

Were we going to crash? Did it even matter? I swore I held my breath and when the wheels finally touched down on the ground, my feet pressed to the floor, as if I were hitting the invisible break. The landing felt different, almost like we couldn't stop.

Screeching, the power of trying to stop pushing on my body and then finally, we did come to a halt.

I exhaled, opened my eyes and looked across the aisle to Will.

"That was rough."

"Tell me about it."

Wren's voice came over the speaker. "Just hang, tight, keep your seatbelts on. I'm going to taxi back over toward the terminal, I saw a boarding staircase there. Not sure what happened, we were met with storm like conditions without a storm. So, I want to move slowly. Sorry about all that."

I looked back at Will. "I think I need one of those drinks your dad is hoarding."

Will chuckled. "You're fine. I wonder what he meant storm like conditions without a storm."

"Wind?"

As the plane slowly taxied and turned, I saw Will do a double take out his window. "Shit. Shit."

"What?"

"Look at that thing."

He was referencing the black wall of whatever it was. In the distance, and it looked like a safe distance, it appeared to be night. Just completely dark. Such a contrast to the sunny day just outside my window. But I didn't see the thing for long or study it, because the plane moved away and toward the terminal.

Turning back around in his seat, Will looked at me. "I think I saw building outlines in there. I think. Maybe it was my imagination."

It would be comforting to believe that. That somehow Will saw buildings in the darkness, that we weren't miles away from the literal end of the world. As if we were in some science fiction movie or book where the world just disappeared.

As far as what it was and what was going on in that area, we'd have to wait until the man called Naples got back to us.

Through my own window I watched as we passed planes half on the runway. One plane was on its side, it had been on fire. The charred remains only. It was no longer smoking or smoldering. Clearly it crashed days earlier. There were other planes near the terminal, waiting I suppose to take off. Then I saw the rolling staircase that Wren spoke of. It was nestled near one of those jet bridges that connected to the plane. I was glad he was going to get that. I didn't want to slide down some emergency ramp, not in my condition.

He guided the craft alongside it and finally brought the plane to a quiet stop.

Ding.

"Did he really turn off the seatbelt sign?" asked Will.

A few seconds later, Wren came from the flight deck with Will behind him.

"So, I don't know what happened. All my gauges read everything was fine," Wren explained. "It was as if I flew through the worst thunderstorm, but once we got close enough to the ground, we broke through whatever it was. Right now, again, I'm getting normal readings. We'll find out."

Trace explained. "Wren is going to go below to get out and get that ladder."

"Then we get off the plane," Wren explained. "We'll maneuver it over to the jet bridge and get into the terminal from there. Then, hopefully hear from Colorado about what's going on. I don't want to get too far away from the plane so we can take off again. Okay?" He waited to see if we had any questions, then he nodded. "I'll be back." He headed to the back of the plane.

Trace walked over and sat by me. "How are you feeling?"

"Sore," I answered.

"We shook a lot. As soon as we can get somewhere with a pharmacy, I'll get you something for the pain."

"I'm fine. Just ibuprofen right now would be a godsend."

"Oh," Emily said. "I can help there." She still wore her purse, a little 'cross the chest' sort of thing and she reached in pulling out a pill box. She handed it to Trace.

"I'll get you some water." He stood.

"I'll get it," Will said. "I need to stand anyhow."

The plane was quiet and I could hear Wren opening a hatch.

Will returned quickly with the water, and I welcomed the ibuprofen. I knew it would take a while to work.

"Thank you," I said. "What's next?"

"Wait until we hear it's safe to go through that," Trace

explained. "Who's to say that dark didn't have anything to do with our rough landing because we're about forty miles from it. I hate, you know, having to go into the terminal. We're on our second day. I don't see any light. So, no air conditioning. It's not going to smell pretty in there. Or look pretty."

"Las Vegas airport shocked me," said Will.

"How so?" Trace asked.

"Dad, we've been through that airport, what? A hundred times? Okay maybe not a hundred. But have you ever seen it so empty? We flew in prime flying time. Vacation time. Where were all the people? I mean it's so crowded you wait forty minutes in line at a burger joint."

"What are you saying?" I asked him.

"I'm saying. The event either killed people or blinded them. Right?" Will replied. "That airport should have been littered with bodies or people needing help."

With a heavy exhale, Trace ran his hand down his face. "You're right. And that municipal building was awfully empty."

"Cars were wrecked on the streets, Dad," Will said. "How many people did we see moving about?"

"It was early in the morning," Trace then shook his head and took a dismissive attitude. "I think we were all in shock and weren't paying attention."

"Dad, come on, you said about the airport …"

"Will. Let it go."

I released an airy chuckle. "Are you trying to stop him from talking so we don't get scared."

"No, actually, I'm not that chivalrous. I'm stopping myself from getting scared." Trace shifted his eyes. "And I need to open the door before I forget what he showed me. Wren is back."

As Trace shuffled away, I looked out my window. That yellow staircase was right against the plane with Wren at the bottom.

"Hey," Will whispered. "Don't let him fool you, he is that chivalrous."

"Maybe he is scared, Will."

Will shrugged. "Who isn't right now."

I heard the door open and Wren's voice.

"See it?" Wren hollered. "Secure it there. No. Not that. That one. Yeah."

"I'm going to go see if my dad needs help." Will left to join his father.

Emily helped me to my feet and assisted me with walking. I didn't need her help, but I thought she needed to do it, so I accepted it.

I realized once I lifted my leg to take that first step, that I was going to fall. Each step was horrendous, piercing pain. I made it down with a brave face and dreaded having to climb back up.

Once we were all on the ground, Wren and Will moved the staircase toward the sky bridge.

I took in the moment, getting some fresh air. But there was a weird smell and feeling to it. Like a stale room closed for the winter.

Maybe it was remnants of the smell coming from the airport.

With precautionary warnings to be careful as I stepped from the staircase to the jet bridge, I moved forward. I was the last, taking the longest. It was just as painful walking up than down.

I was good when I stood and didn't move. I didn't feel the pain from my other injuries because of my ribs. Maybe I wasn't as bad as I thought. Lucky to be alive after being trampled.

The four of them waited at the beginning of the jet bridge for me to get up the steps.

"We'll head in," Wren explained. "Try to find an area with less people or bodies. Just everyone mentally prepare yourselves." He led the way, took a few steps and stopped. "And I know you'll want to, but it's dangerous to help anyone."

Trace added. "We still need to watch out for the ones that were on the plane. The loco ones."

"Loco ones?" Will asked.

"Eh," Trace waved out his hand. "I think using crazy sounds insensitive. They're sick. This is more PC."

Will glanced at me. "I don't think he realizes loco is still insensitive."

I wanted to laugh, but I refrained, knowing it would hurt.

It was warm in the jet bridge and walking down it was walking through a tunnel of the unknown.

There was no noise, no music, no sounds.

We just walked until we arrived at the closed door.

Wren held the handle and looked at us. "Just prepare yourselves."

Trace added. "Even if there isn't a lot of dead, there is going to be a smell."

As a preliminary measure I placed my hand over my nose and mouth.

Wren opened the door.

I didn't hear anything.

I expected noise, groans, those uninterpretable words the affected made.

Nothing.

With the lack of sounds, I braced myself for seeing bodies.

Lots of bodies.

The event hit on a Sunday morning, one of the busiest traveling days of the year.

How many people were in that airport? With that darkness so near to the Oklahoma airport, were things worse there, different?

I heard Trace murmur, "What the hell?" seconds after he stepped through.

I couldn't see until I walked out and into the terminal.

My hand lowered.

It was unnecessary.

Were we in a closed terminal? Perhaps the international side?

Whatever the case, it wasn't what I expected.

It wasn't what any of us expected.

No affected, no dead, no bodies.

Nothing.

Not a single person was there.

Empty.

CHAPTER TWENTY-TWO – TERMINALLY

The thought that we had arrived in an unused terminal or anything like that quickly left my mind. Suitcases, purses, jackets, half eaten food were everywhere. But there were no people.

It wasn't as if they disintegrated into a pile of white dust like some bad 1970s movie. The seats were empty.

But were they? I watched Trace reach down and touch an empty seat.

The crinkle sound caught his attention, mine as well.

Will opened a bag of chips.

"What are you doing?" Trace snapped.

"Seeing if the food tastes weird," Will answered. "If the food tastes weird then Stephen King is a master psychic putting Nostradamus to shame."

"What?" Trace huffed irritated.

Wren softly laughed. "It's not Langoliers."

"Langoliers?" I asked.

Wren spewed forth quickly., "People on a plane land in yesterday, but yesterday is disappearing, breaking down behind them. It's good."

"Ah." I nodded. "I don't think we went to yesterday."

"I don't think so either." Will put the bag of chips down. "They taste fine. But where are all the people?"

Trace answered, "I don't know. But we're not finding out staying here." And then he started to walk.

I didn't know exactly where Trace was leading us because he started walking from the gate, moving as if he had a purpose or direction. Will mentioned something about us being in the expansion section and we probably needed to get to the main terminal.

Whatever that meant. I just followed.

We were wrong about one thing, there was electricity. The lights made the emptiness look less scary. In fact, the electronics hum was the only sound I could hear. The intermittent on and off of the air conditioning.

The terminal and the gate where we arrived was normal looking and like every other airport I had been to. Not that I had been to that many. A long narrow passageway. Gates on both sides. It wasn't until we passed the private lounge that we entered into a wider, long hallway. It seemed like a connection. As we made it halfway through that, I saw what was ahead. Sun. It opened up. It was brighter. The original terminal. It looked huge.

And then I saw something else.

A child.

My heart skipped a beat.

A Child.

A Child alone just sitting there in this big empty airport.

She sat on the floor, crossed legs, on what seemed the edge of the old terminal and the hallway. As if she were the gate keeper.

She was still twenty feet away. Her head slightly lowered, her long dark blonde hair dangled some covering her face. I could see she was still wearing her backpack.

She was small, but not too small or young. I guessed maybe eight years old. As we moved closer, I saw she had food encircling her. Some empty packages and soda cans on their side.

She didn't look disheveled.

She didn't look at all. Not at us or anything.

We all stopped and looked at each other.

She didn't lift her head even as we neared her.

Standing in a line in front of her, six feet maybe, we all were puzzled.

She didn't move.

Will whispered. "Get ready. I think she's one of them."

"One of what?" I asked.

"The loco people like in the plane."

Slowly the child lifted her head and brought her finger to her lips in a 'shhh' sign.

I saw her eyes.

Gray.

She had been blinded but obviously could hear us.

The mother in me rushed forward to her, crouching down.

"Honey, are you okay?" I asked.

"Shh," she said softly. "They'll hear you."

Trace stepped forward. "Who?"

"They'll hear you." And she pointed behind her.

CHAPTER TWENTY-THREE – QUIET

She looked at Trace with such an adult expression. One that seemed annoyed yet laced with a hint of fear.

I didn't understand it.

Why was she telling us to be quiet? It was eerie. A freaky scene from a horror movie. I should have realized why she issued her warning. It was only a few seconds earlier Will had mentioned them. And I didn't think. I was so concerned with the child alone, a child blinded by the event, that I failed to recognize she was somehow smarter and more savvy than I was.

Her lips parted, quivering slightly. "Please,"

She said in the softest of whispers. "Help me."

Instantly my heart broke and Will hurried over and reached down to her. It wasn't until I heard the thunderous sound that I realized Will wasn't grabbing her for comfort. He was doing as she asked.

Saving her.

The sound grew louder and within seconds, hundreds, if not thousands of people ran our way. Following the sound of our voices. I wondered where everyone went and we were about to be greeted by them all.

In the narrow hallway terminal, the view of the open and lower terminal became crowded with affected people.

Will swept the little girl into his arms and charged off in the opposite direction. Back to where we came from.

I was frozen solid.

Unable to move wasn't effecting Trace or Emily. One of them grabbed my arm, pulling me and all I heard was someone yelling out to run.

Run.

When I saw them, the massive amount of them, change our direction, flight or fight kicked in.

There was no way to fight.

Spinning around, I ran.

Will was ahead of all of us. I thought for a moment we were running back to a plane until I saw Wren holding open the private lounge door. Trace ran in, Emily then me.

Will set the little girl down.

Wren closed the glass door and secured the lock.

He looked at all of us with his finger to his lips and ever so softly, said, "Shh."

All of us watched.

The only view we had was through the glass on the door and as we stayed quiet, I watched the massive amount of people run by. Chasing the direction of a sound, but now we were quiet.

I felt safe, but I also knew that they now were in the terminal and getting to our plane would be nearly impossible.

We stood there. Not making a sound. Breathing as shallow as we could.

What was next?

❊ ❊ ❊

"If you don't make noise," said the little girl softly. "They don't come. They can't see like me. But they're angry. They don't know what they're doing. They have to be close to hear. I think. But still talk softly.'

Trace asked her, "What's your name?"

"Haley."

Gently Trace touched the top of her. "Haley, we'll get you out of here. But I'll tell you what? You're so brave."

"Very brave," I added. "It's been two days I don't know how you did it."

I didn't move," she replied. "I peed my pants."

"Me, too," I replied.

Will with a snicker looked at me. "Did you really?"

I mouthed the words "shut up" with a scolding look then said, "I did and so did you." Turning from the girl, I saw the expression on Emily's face. She seemed shocked, maybe even a little sad looking at her.

Wren stood by the door, trying to see out. I walked over to him.

"Anything?"

Wren shook his head. "Let's see if they hear this." He slowly turned the lock on the door.

it clicked.

We waited.

They didn't come.

"I say we go," Trace approached us. "Get out of the airport."

"And go where?" I asked. "Back to the plane?"

Wren shook his head. "That's not a possibility if we want to go East. I mean. We can make a noise and lead them away but we can't fly until we hear from Naples and he tells us what was going on in the darkness."

"Obviously the world is there," Trace said. "It didn't break off."

Emily rushed to us. "We can't stay in the airport. But with those things out there."

"People," Trace snapped. "They were affected by whatever happened and I'm not convinced until I see a brain scan that this thing isn't temporary."

"I'll see again?" Haley asked softly and innocently.

"I hope."

"Dad," Will harshly whispered. "You can't tell a kid something like that until you know. You don't know."

"I know this," Trace said. "I know nothing scientifically that can cause this. Or natural that would make this happen."

Haley spoke up. "That's because God did this."

"Haley, honey," I walked over to her. "Why are you saying that?"

"That's what the man said," she replied. "He told the people that could see and they left."

"They left you?" I asked.

"He said I wasn't chosen. But they gave me food and told me to stay quiet."

Wren ran his hand over his face. "So, there's other people out there. Like us."

Haley asked. "You mean chosen?"

"No," Wren replied. "Lucky. And I intend for us to stay that way. But for the moment, until we figure out the next step. We stay here."

And then it was quiet again. Our whispers ceased. Emily sat down still staring at Haley. Will paced and Trace walked to the bar. He had that look on his face, like he was in total thought. He brought some water over to Haley and sat down with her. Wren stayed by that door, as if waiting for something to happen.

I didn't understand the waiting. Sitting there in silence. Those maddened people or Locos were only coming if we made noise.

They didn't hear our whispers, they didn't run by the door again. If they were why we didn't move, if they were the problem in our leaving then we needed to face that problem. But first we needed to know exactly what we faced.

I reached for the door.

Wren stopped me. "What the hell are you doing?"

"I need to know what they're doing. Where they are," I replied. "I'll be quiet. I'll be back."

"I'll go with you."

"No." I shook my head. "I'll go alone." Ever so slowly, I pushed open the door, just enough for me to slip out.

And I did.

Wren eased the door back into the closed position so it wouldn't make a sound.

I looked at him through the glass on the other side of the door.

What the hell was I thinking?

Was I scared? Absolutely.

But I was now out there alone and I had to do what I said I was going to do.

I turned to the direction where the Locos ran and started to walk that way.

CHAPTER TWENTY-FOUR – THE RUSH

I was never brave. I hid my face at every scary movie, fast forwarded over the stressful parts, and immediately picked up my phone while watching a show to find out what would happen, if the tension was too much. Yet, there I was. In that terminal alone venturing out to find out what the affected were doing, what they did when they didn't have a sound to go after that made them act insane.

Even though it wasn't, it felt like a mile long walk.

My heart raced, I cringed with every step I took. What was I thinking?

A part of me felt fine, fearless, that as long as I remained quiet, I would be okay.

I kept thinking about what Trace said. How it could be temporary?

Something happened that hit the brain. Some could see but not hear, some could hear but not see, some lost both. And then there were the Locos. Driven by something that made them angry, striking out.

Granted I had only seen the behavior on the plane. For all I knew, what they did to Mary was a one off.

A glitch of the human reaction.

It was a chance I couldn't take, after all they came in a rampage after us when they heard us.

Passing us by when we drew silent.

The farther I walked away from the lounge and to the area

where we came from, the more I heard them.

They made this noise, a crying noise, almost screaming in pain for help. It wasn't loud, but a steady sound of, which I could only think was the sound of agony.

They were in pain.

The pain could have been what caused them to strike out. Find that sound, not think reasonably and just attack.

When I reached the end of the connection hallway that led to the extension terminal, I saw them all.

Crammed into the one terminal area, engulfing all of the gates.

Their necks were arched back and they moved aimlessly, bumping into one another. Crying out, while heads raised as if to the heavens.

They were lost souls, looking for an answer.

So many of them, blocked the gate that we came from. It wasn't because they had some keen insight, it was because they needed something to follow.

I imagined in time, should they remain like that, they would find a way.

Life ... finds a way.

But my worry was more about how they would live, how they would survive. Surely, they weren't eating or drinking anything.

The human body can only go so long without food or water.

They were all human, not some undead wandering the earth. I felt sorry for them, instinctively moving toward the noise.

They didn't see me. As long as I didn't make a sound, they wouldn't know I was there, and if I did make a sound and they raced towards it, I wondered if I would be safe hiding or did they suddenly develop a heightened sense of smell?

Physically I was in no condition to run. I stayed there for a few moments studying them. Wondering again if what I witnessed on the plane was just the immediate ramifications.

I wasn't willing to find out.

They were blocking our way out. If we ventured from the lounge we could get out of the airport if we were quiet.

Or we make a distraction noise that they would chase and we go back to the plane.

That would be my choice on what to do and I was going to suggest it.

After I felt I had seen enough, quietly I made my way back toward the lounge and stood at the door until Wren saw me and let me in.

"We'll?" he asked.

"They're all crammed down by the gate we came in," I replied. "Not really moving, they seem like they're waiting."

"For a noise?"

"Maybe. But I think if we're quiet, we can find a way to draw them away from the gate and the other way. Giving us an opening to get back to the plane."

"And fly where?" Wren asked. "We don't know what's in the darkness. Do you want to take that chance?"

"I want to go home."

"I get that. Maybe fly to Colorado."

"That is the total opposite way from where I want to go."

Trace inched to us. "Haley said a man came and took people. Maybe we should find them."

"Why?" I tossed out my hands, still keeping my voice down. "They left a child."

"He obviously led people that weren't affected. So that means more like us are out there."

"Is this the doctor in you or the man, that so desperately wants to find an answer."

"Both."

"Look,". Wren said. "I know one thing. We can't stay in this lounge. We have to go and we have to get a hold of Colorado somehow to see if they figured out the darkness. I don't know if the towers went down or we just don't have a signal. I wanna get you home Shelb. But I need to know what's East."

I nodded. "Okay. So, let's get out of here and find somewhere we can get that answer. An area with a signal or phone. We have his number."

Every word I spoke was in desperation, I was motivated selfishly to find my family. To get to them.

If they were in the dark and silence, I had to lead them out of it, but we were going on three days since the event.

I held hope they were able to survive. Others have, but for how long?

CHAPTER TWENTY-FIVE – RIDICULOUS

We were repeating ourselves. Nothing new. Not that we all had been doing the same thing forever, but it seemed redundant.

Heading out of the airport our plan was to find a van or something ... again. Just like we did in Las Vegas. Then head into another city ... again. Look for others ... again, and not to forget the answers Trace led us to look for.

Would this happen everywhere we went?

I just wanted to go home. Every time I thought of my children and husband my heart ached. I wanted to bury myself in denial, believing they were fine.

How could they be?

Almost everyone in the world was affected.

The world went silent and we were wading through it in a search for something we would never find an answer to, because there were none.

We left the lounge and moved quietly. No one spoke or made a sound. We just didn't know about the locos and what they would do. Trace and Will communicated, because they both were fluent in sign language.

I had no idea what they were saying.

The original and main terminal was beautiful and large, we aimed for the escalator. I could see the sign ahead.

But Will noticed something else. He waved out his arm to get our attention then pointed to a set of double glass doors, then signed something to his father.

Trace replied with an agreeing look. Whatever Will said must have been a good idea.

I wasn't sure about this being a good idea. The doors were oddly placed because I knew we were on a second level.

They weren't gate doors. The authorized personnel only sign told me very little.

Wren nodded then made his way over to them. After looking out, he pulled on the door very slowly.

It opened.

He then told us in a signal wave of his hand to come to him.

What were we going to do? Jump?

Will lifted Haley and walked toward the door.

She could have walked herself, but I think he carried her more because of what was on the other side.

I hated thinking about how that little girl felt. Walking in the dark, alone and not knowing where she was.

I didn't know her story, how she came to be at the airport, or what she was doing when it happened.

The closer I walked to the double doors, the more the white stairs could be seen.

We would be out of the terminal earlier than if we had gone the original way we had planned. We were actually going to be closer to the plane. Theoretically we could fly out.

I just wanted to get out, stop trying to be so quiet.

It was unnerving.

Any sound could draw the Locos.

Wren held the door open.

Ring.

It wasn't just a ring it was a ring tone. Frank Sinatra's 'That's Life' blasted through the silence.

I wasn't expecting it, I jumped.

Emily peeped a shriek in her startle.

"Whose phone?" Haley asked. "Someone has a phone."

Will placed her down, reached for his phone and silenced it.

Trace blasted out a harsh, "Shhh."

We all shut up.

A second, maybe three and that thunderous sound of running grew louder.

A stamped. We had to get out of there fast, and we did.

We hurried through the door, standing on those stairs I watched as all those people almost ran by us again.

They had an idea where the sound came from because they didn't stop far from where we had made our escape.

Once we all made it down the stairs, Wren started checking the vans that were parked there, while Will checked his phone.

"Was it them?" Trace asked. "From Colorado?"

"Yeah," Will replied. "I'll call them back."

"Wait until we get one of these vans and put us on speaker so we all can hear."

"Can't we go to the plane?" I asked.

Trace slightly huffed. "Did you not notice how hard of a time we had landing. We went through something we couldn't see. What makes you think taking off will work?"

"Wow, no need to huff." I shook my head.

"Found one," Wren asked.

I mumbled under my breath. "Great. Now we drive somewhere else."

Emily gently spoke to me. "I know you want to go home. You'll get there."

Wren opened the door for me. "We need to find out what's there. Let's call them back."

I nodded then it hit me. I didn't notice at first, maybe it was my adrenaline or attitude, but it was cold. Really cold out.

We all loaded into the van, Wren and I in the front. Trace, Will, Emily and Haley in the back.

Will sat closer to the front and dialed his phone. He had it on the speaker and the line thrilled.

"Cleveland, hey," said Naples, when he picked up the line. "I got worried when you didn't answer."

"We were in a situation," Will replied. "We couldn't answer."

"Do you have any news?" Wren asked.

"We have theories, based on what we have seen from the

drone and learned. They're pretty good," Naples stated. "Not the circumstances, but the theories."

"Can I go home," I blurted out. "I live south of Cleveland."

"Can we do video call?" he asked. "I'd like to see who I'm talking to before the cell lines go down. We'll have phones for a while, but cells, like the power is going to go soon."

"Give me a sec, I'll call you right back," Will disconnected the call and started calling him with a video call.

I sensed a stare from Trace and looked over to him. "What?"

"Can you wait until the man is done explaining before you ask anything?"

Was I really that unnerving to him? His attitude increasingly became irritated.

Wait until the man is done? He said.

When I saw the video, Naples was closer to a boy. He was young, fair skinned with a buzz, military cut. It was dark where he was, a few people moved about in the back. All military. He had to be scared, he was so young. Probably not even old enough to drink. At least to me he looked it.

"So good to see your faces," Naples said. "So, guys, look, the drone went into the dark zone. It went from New York City to Philadelphia, so I can't say what's beyond that. I can tell you what we saw. No signs of destruction, no signs of people. There were, however, many casualties. We can confirm that what happened was some sort of cosmic event. It struck in that zone. But not New York or Philly."

Wren looked around at us then spoke up, "Explain cosmic event and why you think that."

"A solar flare, CME, something. It struck the region that's now dark. We believe that fully. And from those who survived the event outside of the dark area," said Naples, "They described a bright light."

Trace added. "Something so bright it instantly blinded them. Similar to the don't look at an eclipse."

"Or nuclear flash," Naples said. "But yes. And to affect the hearing, thought process and so on, there had to have been some sort of sonic sound."

Trace stated, "Which would explain why those wearing ear buds were spared, but ... How did it affect the brain? Has any doctor done an MRI or CT scan for a brain bleed or damage."

"There are several doing testing now, but they had to go into the city for the equipment."

I had been sitting up some and when I heard them talking my body just sat back in defeat. "I saw it. I saw the flash. I thought it was interference on my phone. The entire screen with my family went white. I was doing video messenger in the bathroom of the plane. My husband was warning me and here I thought he was being some jealous asshole because I was going away. But he was warning me." I turned my head back to the phone. "Was there a warning?"

Naples hesitated to answer. "Something was seen maybe eight minutes before it happened, but no one knew what it was and where it was going to strike."

Emily exhaled loudly with almost a gasp. "Eight minutes, how were people supposed to get to safety in that time let alone comprehend what was happening?"

Wren answered, "They weren't. There wasn't enough time. So could people be alive in that area?"

"It's not as black as it seems," replied Naples. "One of the guys here has a good analogy. Ever drive down a flat highway and see a storm ahead? You can see the rain, right, you know it's there because it looks like a gray wall. That's why the dark looks so dark. Once the drone was in there, it was like nighttime without lights or stars or a moon. Just dark. Wherever it hit is gone. We just can't see right now."

Will asked. "What do you mean gone."

"When the CME or flare hit, it was probably like the biggest nuke known to man. It sent shock waves across the globe."

"The massive drop in the plane," Will said. "That was caused by it?"

"Yep," Naples said. "But guys, there's something you should know." He paused. "It's highly radiated in there. In fact, I would suggest heading over to Tinker and finding a Geiger counter or radiation meter. Something to gauge radiation because you're awfully close to it."

"Tinker isn't far at all," Wren said. "Have you had any contact with them?"

"None. Doesn't mean someone isn't there, it's only been a couple days."

"How long?" I asked. "How long will it be radiated?"

"We don't know, levels could drop in a couple weeks."

I don't know what was said in the rest of that phone call, but upon hearing that, filled with a sense of failing desperation, immediately, I opened the van door and got out. I needed to catch my breath. My heart raced out of control, I could feel the wave of grief hitting me. My emotions were so out of check that I didn't feel any pain from my ribs.

It kept racing through my mind. My last phone call with my family.

The white flash I saw.

How stupid, incredibly stupid I was. I was so consumed with fighting with my husband I didn't listen to what he said.

That flash.

My family was there in the middle of it.

They were in that area that was unsafe. What was I supposed to do? Not go looking for them for two weeks? It wasn't an option. If they were affected, they needed me. Plain and simple, I didn't care about anything if my family was no longer alive. And every day that passed where they didn't have help was another day they stood a chance of leaving me.

"Shelb," Will called my name and came from the van. "Are you okay?"

"No. No, I'm not."

"I'm sorry this wasn't the news you wanted."

"It's the news I needed to hear, right? Did I miss something worse when I got out?"

"No. We did tell them about Haley and what she said about

the man."

Emotionally I chuckled. "Let me guess, after we go to whatever this Tinker store is …"

"Base," Will corrected.

"What?"

"Tinker is an air force base."

"Oh, great, so we go to Tinker and look for these people. That's the plan, right?" Before he answered I noticed Will's eyes drifted behind me. I looked back over my shoulder, Wren and Trace had stepped from the van.

"There's enough gas," Wren said. "We can make it to Tinker, but I don't think the highway is an option."

"I don't want to go." I shook my head.

"There's a clinic at Tinker," added Trace. "I can do an Xray on you. Make sure everything is alright."

"I'm fine." I snapped.

Trace continued as if I didn't say anything, "Also give Haley a once over properly." He paused. "Wanna say she's fine, too?"

I pursed my lips. "I know I'm being difficult."

"And I get that," Trace replied. "I understand it, I do. But understand, we are limited in what we can do. Going to Tinker is a great option."

"I don't want to go."

"You don't have a choice," said Trace.

I heaved a breath of shock. "What do you mean?"

"You're part of this group."

"I didn't ask to be part of the group."

"Too bad."

"Okay," Wren interjected. "We're in this together whether we like it or not. Safety in numbers."

"Really, because a single person is quieter than a collective group?"

"Will you stop?" Trace barked. "I would think you of all people would want to find answers like the rest of us."

"You got your answers Trace," I said. "You know what happened and why. What more do you need to know?"

Trace stammered his answer with a bit of sarcasm. "I don't know, maybe how long this will last. Is there permanent damage to those hurt? Is that dark gonna spread? What can we do to survive and keep surviving? Stuff like that."

"Well, I want a different answer. I want to know if my kids are alive and my husband. I'm not going to find it staying this far away."

Trace pointed to the dark in the distance. "You really think going in there is going to tell you what your heart already knows."

"Dad!" Will snapped. "Stop, okay. Both of you just stop. I hear what she's saying. She has to know. If you were in there, I'd want to know. If I was there, I'm sure you'd want to know as well. Quit fighting, everyone. No one is a prisoner in this group." He faced me. "Look, Shelb, you do what you need to do."

"Oh my god," Trace said. "Are you telling her to go to Cleveland?"

"I'm telling her to do what she wants."

"I want to go home," I said softly.

"We can't put the group in that position," Trace spoke gently. "We have a little girl with us. It's dangerous."

"I'll go alone, I'm okay with that."

Trace shook his head and walked away, getting back into the van.

"I've promised you I'd get you home." Wren told me. "I'll go with you if you want. Whatever you choose. But let's go to Tinker and get supplies?"

I nodded. "Yeah, let's do that."

Wren reached out, placing a hand on my shoulder, then went back to the van.

I faced Will. "Am I being ridiculous? Tell me."

"Yeah, but," he shrugged. "It doesn't matter. What matters is you get the answers and truth you need to get. That's not being ridiculous, it's being human in a desperate situation. I can safely say," Will said. "We're all being that way."

"Except Haley."

Tight lipped, Will smiled. "Except Haley."

Maybe I was missing something. All of us adults were scattered with emotions and agendas. Agendas for the good of the group, some not.

Haley, however, said very little.

Maybe because I didn't know her or perhaps didn't listen.

It was time I did.

CHAPTER TWENTY-SIX – OKLAHOMA STORMS

"My mom, dad and brother," Haley told us as we drove in the van. "We were waiting to go to Disneyland."

"So, you live in Oklahoma City?" I asked.

"Yes."

"Haley," Trace asked. "Do you remember when it all happened?"

Haly nodded. "I was playing on my tablet and it just got so bright."

"Did you feel anything?" Trace question. "Did your eyes burn, anything?"

"Not at first, then they did after I couldn't see. I screamed for my mom. I didn't hear her. People were making noise, like crying and I couldn't see. I cried, too."

"I bet," Trace said. "Do you remember anything else?"

"I was crying. I heard some man calling out for Linda. I called out to him. I called out for help. He came over. He asked where his wife went. She was right by the window. She was gone. He said she was gone and then he walked away calling for her."

"Was this the same man that took people away?" Trace asked.

"I don't think so."

Will whispered in almost discovery. "She was by the window. Those windows are huge."

"What are you getting at?" Trace asked.

"Haley," Will said. "Where were you when this all happened?"

"By the bathroom near the gate," she answered. "There was nowhere to sit."

"Dad," Will said. "Do you think it's possible that anyone fully exposed was …"

"Vaporized?" Trace cut him off. "From the flash? Possible, that could explain the missing people."

"Linda was missing," said Haley. "It was quiet for a while then the man came. He told me he was sorry I wasn't chosen and to stay quiet. He gave me food. What is vaporized?"

Emily gently explained. "It's a way of saying they disappeared suddenly."

"Like God took them?" Haley asked. "The man said that. He said God took people, left the chosen and something about the rest of us."

I was too busy listening to Haley and looking back that I didn't notice the rain sound that pelted against the metal roof of the van, not until Wren said something.

"Holy crap this weather is bad." Wren leaned into the steering wheel to try to peer out at the sky.

It was dark and threatening. Lightning flashed like I had never seen. I had heard about the storms in Oklahoma, how they were unlike anywhere else in the world, and from what I witnessed that was not an exaggeration.

It was crazy.

It went from calm and overcast to insane weather. Sideways rain and wind that moved the van.

We had taken the long way, avoiding the highway. Even the streets were riddled with cars, creating a maze that Wren navigated through. But with the water landing on the windshield like buckets of water, driving was impossible.

Surely, we would hit something.

As soon as Wren proclaimed we would wait it out in the van and that it was safe, a street sign flew at smashing into the front end of the van before bouncing off and flying away.

"Maybe not," Wren said.

"We need to get inside somewhere," I said, then pointed. "What about that?"

Clearly it was a church, but we were on a side street facing a small building attached to the church. The offices perhaps.

There was a fence and on the other side was a little path that led to a covered porch. The gate of the fence swung violently in the weather.

"Once I open the door," Trace said. "We make a run for it. Will, do you have Haley?"

"I'll grab her."

"Shelb, are you okay to run?" he asked me.

"I'll bring up the rear, but I'll make it."

"Everyone remember. We go in there, we stay quiet because we don't know who might be there."

Trace counted it down. Three, two, one. When he slid open the door, the rain was even louder.

I was joking at first about bringing up the rear, but I was the last one out of the van.

The rain was cold and heavy, hitting my face, making it impossible to see correctly. I was drenched by the time I arrived, last, at the porch.

I wiped my eyes, cleared them of the blurriness and saw the sign. "Rectory Hours'.

Trace tried the door, it was unlocked and he opened it.

We stepped inside into a small office with one desk and another door directly on the opposite wall.

"This is good," I said. "This will work until it stops."

"Shh," Trace told me.

"Dad," Will whispered, then pointed to the other door.

Trace nodded and Will walked to it and then through.

I tossed up my hands. Why were we exploring? Were we going to be there that long? Just until the storm was over.

A few seconds later, Will returned. He spoke softly. "It's a whole thing back there. But it's dark. Can't see a foot in front on me."

Wren patted his hip. "I have one small flashlight."

Emily fumbled with her bag. "I have more. We have them in the go bag." As she reached the bag dropped to the floor causing a 'thump'.

Everyone froze and stood there, waiting.

No sounds. No running. For the time being we were safe.

<><><>

Passing through that door was like walking into one of those haunted houses. At any moment something could jump out.

It was impossible to see anything even with the flashlights Emily had passed out. I of course, didn't get one, because I bragged I had my own.

But I didn't.

I couldn't see a thing. I was feeling around for a light switch, something to help me. Like an idiot, I left my flashlight outside in the small office with my wet bag. Totally forgetting I didn't have it on my person. By the time I reached for it, I was inside the dark hallway. A long dark hallway. Behind me it was black. We all entered, where did the others go? It was only a hallway.

But I was there and couldn't see anyone.

I felt alone. There had to be a light switch.

Walking down the hall, something or someone reached for me. It took everything I had not to scream at the touch that came out of the darkness.

The fingertips were cold when they reached out, grazing against my arm. I couldn't tell if it was a man or a woman, they didn't grab me, just reaching for me.

One finger, two. As if to say, 'who is there'?

There were people there in that building, I could sense it, probably seeking refuge from the rain or rather just seeking refuge.

Like me.

Only my refuge wasn't some spiritual one, it was a dry and warmth one.

I pushed away the person.

Did the group finally have enough of me? I heard no one behind me.

A few more steps and I caught the beam of Trace's flashlight. I saw it swishing back and forth. Finally, it was as if he just put it on. It was a church rectory, it couldn't be that big.

I hurried to catch up to him just as he made a quick right turn.

Then finally, it wasn't dark.

We were in a small office, nobody was in there. The name plate on the desk read, *The most Reverand Donald Birch.* The office was filled with books, religious ornaments and the small statue of the blessed mother told me more than likely, we were in a Catholic Church.

There was a sense of comfort in that room.

Trace swirled his finger, then fist closed pointed to the side with his extended thumb. I knew he was asking where the others were.

He was using sign language again, something I hadn't seen him use since the plane.

I shrugged. I wasn't sure if they were ahead of me or behind. After all, in a blind let's make a deal moment, we all had different doors to choose.

He sighed out lowering his shoulders. He then signed for me to wait behind and he started to leave the office.

Shaking my head 'no', I grabbed his arm and gave him a hard look that spoke volumes that I wasn't staying behind alone. I wasn't some damsel in distress, I just didn't want to stay there alone.

I didn't want to trip or fall, I was already feeling pain with every step.

I was sure there were no Locos in the church. Even if they were hard to see in the dark, I could hear them.

They would have come already. Thank God they didn't. We

were trapped.

Trace waved his flashlight for me to follow him. The hall was a bit brighter with that office light on, but that would fade.

We continued down the hall and the beam of the flashlight shone a bigger door. It was cliché in a church doorway. As Trace reached for it, a shuffle and a thump behind us caught my attention.

I turned, as did Trace and his flashlight met the beam of another.

"Shit," It was Will.

Both Trace and I did the signature, 'shh'.

"I don't know what I tripped over."

Again, we both quietly said, 'shh'.

Will lowered his flashlight. A man was in the hall, just sitting there on the floor, another stood by him.

Probably the person that reached to touch me.

"Sorry, Dude."

Trace rushed by me to his son.

"What?" Will asked. "He's harmless."

He made the signal asking where the others were.

In a whisper, Will answer. "They found a kitchen. I was looking for …"

'Shh.'

"Oh my God," Will gasped softly. "There are no Locos here."

Trace, in such a father manner snapped his finger and pointed to behind Will.

Will barely spoke the word, but the way his mouth formed it, he replied with, "Fine."

Trace stepped away.

"What are you looking for anyhow?" Will asked. "We found a good spot. With food."

Even though I saw only Trace's back, I could tell by the way he breathed out, he was getting frustrated. Intervening, I tugged on Trace's shirt and waved him to move away and for us to continue.

Almost deliberately, in a child challenging a parent moment, it seemed as if Will waited until Trace started to walk away when he said, "I'll go have Spam."

I stopped Trace and pointed ahead.

Like Will, I really didn't understand where we were going or the point of moving onward. Will said they found a kitchen and it was a good place.

Why did Trace want to keep going?

The only thing I could figure was curiosity.

He needed to see. He needed to know.

It was something I was learning about Trace. He always needed to know and find answers. Maybe it was the scientist in him.

He couldn't just sit in a place, have some Spam and move onward at first light. He had to look through every inch of a place.

Like he wanted to with the church.

We made our way back to that big old door. There was some hesitation when Trace reached for it.

He knew where it led and I did, too.

It had to be one place.

The church.

I stayed close to him not wanting to be in the dark if he stepped in there and got too far ahead of me.

The office light still carried to us, but it wouldn't once we passed through that old door.

It creaked at a high pitch as Trace pushed it open, but a sound wasn't the only thing that carried to me. People noises, crying, coughing, murmuring voices.

The door was a barrier of sound among other things. Keeping it all in there tucked away. Once opened it unleashed the horror.

Smells.

An immediate smell.

It wasn't death, I had smelt that. This was a more common smell that we encountered.

A sour smell of urine, feces and vomit.

It was overwhelming, replacing the church scent of incense.

It wafted in the air, hit my nose, traveled to my throat and inflamed my glands causing my mouth to immediately fill with saliva as I fought desperately the repeated gags that hit me.

Don't throw up, don't throw up. I told myself.

The echoing effect as we stepped through told me more than what I could see.

We definitely were in the church, on the altar.

Judging by the exterior of the church, one flashlight wasn't big enough.

As we walked forward, the light shed on a pulpit, then a communion table, then somewhere mid altar we stopped.

I heard the shuffling, movement of people, muted conversations with words popping out louder then soft. No volume control.

They were communicating.

It was different.

But there was crying. So much crying.

Trace faced the sounds and slowly moved his flashlight forward.

As I thought, there were people there.

People sought comfort and it made sense they would go to a church.

They were crammed in there, some moved about bumping into things, others sat in the pews.

I didn't know what the church looked like in the day, but in the dark, with minimal daylight and stormy skies, through the illumination of a flashlight, it was dismal.

There were more people than I thought, helpless and hopeless, like everywhere else.

How did they get there? How did they find their way there?

I couldn't have. If it were me without eyes or ears, I wouldn't move.

Maybe the desire to live and survive drove them to move and they found the church.

I didn't understand it.

"It's amazing that they all made their way in here," I said. "Following faith."

"Not really," answered Trace. "It was Sunday, they were here when it happened."

I didn't even think about that. How they followed their faith before the event and were there, unable to do anything now but sit and cry and ponder their fate, while praying.

Or did they stop praying.

After swinging his light back and forth, Trace saw all he needed or wanted to see. With a quick grab of my arm, he signaled it was time to go.

I looked back once more, not that I could see anything.

Suddenly it was dark again.

Black.

As if nothing was there, an emptiness, a void.

But the reality was, I could walk away from the void of darkness.

It wasn't permanent for us.

In the light of day or even through the beam of a flashlight or flicker of a candle, the darkness was breached.

We could see and hear where we were headed.

Unfortunately, the reality was, for those in the church and for those who survived and were marred by the event, that wasn't the case.

We headed back to find the others.

CHAPTER TWENTY-SEVEN – BLIND EYE

The smell was reminiscent of being a teenager, engrossed in my grandmother's cooking and love of Spam. It was a weird smell, but a better smell than what we had just dealt with at the church.

Even though we were safely inside, I could still hear the rain and storm outside.

I stepped into the kitchen of the rectory. It was old-fashioned with yellow paint. The kitchen cabinets were old white metal ones and Emily stood at the stove.

There was a big oval table in the middle, Wren, Will and Haley sat there.

"I wish there was a door to shut this off," Trace said then sat at the table. "We'll take shifts keeping an eye out. Stay here as long as we can until the weather breaks. If it's dark we stay until first light."

I tried not to let my disappointment show as I joined them at the table. "Any calls from Colorado?" I asked Will.

"Not since earlier," he answered. "They'll keep in contact. They need Wren since he's a pilot. And they did say they got in touch with Mallory at Nellis. Which is good."

"I have a question," Haley spoke up.

"What is it sweetie?" I asked.

"The man on the phone said something from the sun hit our country, right?" she asked. "A solar flare. I know what that is, we learned about that in science."

"Alright," I said.

"Well, it's not day on the other side of the world. If the sun did something, wouldn't it only do something where it is shining?"

"Wow," Wren whispered out. "That makes sense. I didn't think of that. It hit where it was daylight. New York would have been what? Noon?"

"So, what about those on the other side of the world?" I asked. "Would they know, would they be hit?"

Emily set a plate of food down before Haley. Then explained the plate as she placed a fork in her hand. "The man said that the shock was felt around the globe, and they were in touch with the International Space Station. I would think they would know up there. And get in touch down below."

Trace added. "That's if communications weren't knocked out, which is possible. But this isn't the 1800s like the Carrington Incident, they'll get it back. The question is, will they come over and help?"

Will asked. "Would we? I think we would send military over to see what was up."

Wren added. 'The ISS will give them information if they already haven't."

Haley fiddled trying to eat her food. "Why didn't the man on the radio say anything about it. I mean he's supposed to be smart."

"Sweetie." I reached out laying my hand on her arm. "It's all new. We may know more tomorrow or the next day."

"Speaking of tomorrow," Wren walked over to the window. "It's not getting better and it's already pushing five. We stay here for the night and hit Tinker tomorrow. Sorry about that, Shelb."

I slowly shook my head. "I understand and I need to get to Tinker, too. I want to get what I need. Maybe since you were in the military Wren, you can explain the radiation detector to me."

"You're going in?" Wren asked.

"I'm going in. Or try," I replied. "I just need to get everything

I need."

* * *

While the intensity of the storm let up some, it still rained. I found my spot on the sofa, staring out the window. I didn't want to sleep. Not with so many people in the church. I knew they were injured, but it still was unnerving. Trace stayed in the hallway just outside the living quarters for the priests. He kept watch and that helped me feel somewhat at ease.

I curled up in a sitting position on the corner of the couch. Haley was asleep next to me. Her pillow pushed on my thigh and I often found myself touching her hair, maybe comfort for her or myself. Staring out that window, I kept thinking of my family, how it was another night away from them.

I searched deep within my soul for something, anything to hold onto that they were still alive. I didn't care if they were affected by the event, I wanted them alive.

In the darkness of the night, Emily came in. I thought she was sleeping in the other room. She sat in the chair near the end of the couch.

She stared at me, as if wanting to say something.

Then finally, she broke the silence.

"I know what I did," she said. "In your mind was unforgiveable."

"It's hard to imagine what you did. But it's not for me to judge you. I don't hate you, Emily. I don't understand your decision. It angered me at first. But I am not, yet, faced with seeing my family like that. I can't say I wouldn't do it. I can say that because I don't know."

"You'll find out their fate soon, I believe it," Emily replied. "I would like to go with you."

"I don't want to put anyone in danger. Wren wants to go, but that's because he made a promise, I am not making him keep."

"Danger," Emily breathed out a sort of laugh. "I'm dying Shelby. I went for the MRI so they could do surgery. I know what this tumor is and how aggressive it is. I wasn't going to do anything at first. Funny the timing of me changing my mind huh. Without treatment, which now I won't get, I have a year at most. Six good months. Radiation or an area that's dangerous, I don't care. Let me go with you."

I just stared at her. Admittedly, having someone there wasn't a bad idea.

"I promise, once we find your family. I'll go off somewhere. I really need a purpose for what remains of my life."

I wanted to tell her that she took away her purpose when she killed her family. Before those words slipped from my mouth, it dawned on me, if she stayed to take care of them, they would never know she was dying. Hearing her struggles, until one day, she was gone. She had implied that before, I guess I didn't listen.

"When we find my family, you don't have to leave." I told her. "I'm not that brave, Emily. I'm not. I just know I'm determined."

"We go together. After we get to Tinker, get what we need, we'll leave. Find a vehicle and leave."

"Thank you."

She stood, nodded and smiled gently. "Good night, Shelby."

"Night."

After she left the room, I glanced down at Haley. I wondered who would take care of her, if Trace and Will would be fine with her. I knew they planned to go to Colorado. Maybe there would be people there who could watch Haley.

The poor child.

She lost everything and her sight.

Yet, she was braver than I was.

A part of me felt guilty that I was leaving her, even though I had just met her.

The mother in me wanted to protect her, but the mother in me needed to find my own children.

I would explain it to her, not that it mattered to her, but it mattered to me.

In that short span of time after the conversation with Emily, the weather picked up again. The rain intensified, lightning flashed and blasts of thunder popped off like fireworks.

I told myself I wasn't going to sleep, that I would stare out the window all night.

But I was tired and I eventually dozed off.

It was the rest my body needed for what lay ahead.

CHAPTER TWENTY-EIGHT – TINKER ABOUT

A part of me forgot that Trace had a problem. It was the reason he lost his license and he dismissed it as if it were something as simple and misunderstood as Wren having a nightcap in his hotel room.

It wasn't. My first encounter with him, he drank.

And in the morning, when I woke up, and I saw Will forcefully nudging Trace to get up, I realized he was a functioning alcoholic until he wasn't. A bottle lay by his side along with two airline bottles.

"No worries," Wren said as he walked by me. "I took over watch last night. Did you sleep well?"

"Um, yeah," I stared down at Trace.

"How are you feeling?"

"Better actually. It only really hurt when I first moved." Again, I glanced down to Trace. "Should we make him coffee?" I asked Will.

"He'll be fine once he's up."

"Is he always like this?"

"Every night he can be. He tried you know, yesterday, not to drink. That's why he was so difficult to get along with yesterday."

"What about you?" I asked. "How are you doing?"

"My addiction is a little easier to keep in check. You can't grab my DOC from anywhere."

"DOC?"

"Drug of choice," Will answered.

I nodded. "Are you guys okay to handle Haley when I take off to find my family?"

"I'll be fine," Will replied. "I will be. Haley is in good hands."

I glanced down at Trace.

"She'll be fine," he repeated.

Figuring at that moment I would leave him to get his father roused, I headed to the kitchen. I could smell eggs cooking.

It made me sad. If I could smell the food so could everyone around us. Those poor people in the church. They weren't eating, they weren't drinking. They not only were blinded and deafened by the event, but they also faced a painful, agonizing death and there weren't enough of us who were healthy to help them.

I could sense the silence. Feel it more in the daylight.

Those in that church would remain there until they died. While we moved on.

What a mess.

The world was a mess.

We all were.

Trace lying on the floor in a post binge state reminded me that we were all humans with our faults. This wasn't a perfect scenario, like some movie or book where the heroes were perfect.

The world was falling apart and the beat down it emotionally dealt us wasn't going to be handled with valor.

It would be handled in a way we could cope.

We wouldn't keep our heads held high and bravely face the present and future with strength.

We'd get through it however we could.

Alcohol.

Drugs.

Mercy killing.

We all had coping mechanisms.

Mine was believing I could make it home. I was obsessive and consumed that belief as much as Trace consumed his booze.

It was how we coped.

No right or wrong.

We just had to get through. And my journey was far from over. In hours our little group would go separate ways and I was scared to death of what was ahead for me.

※ ※ ※

The morning light brought about the visual devastation of the storm. Outside the church, debris was scattered about everywhere and also bodies.

There were so many bodies.

It made me sick and my heart hurt. They were lost souls out in the elements with no way to find shelter, prey to the merciless weather that pounded at them.

And what of the ones like the eight on the plane or the ones in the airport. Strong and driven, were they victims to the elements as well or did they have the ability somehow to get away?

The weather we experienced the day before was like a violent cleansing, an unfair cleansing, giving some no choice but for their lives to be washed away.

I could only imagine the horror they felt, hearing nothing, seeing nothing, but feeling the impact.

Scared, alone. A tragedy.

If they were out in the open, they probably would just move until they couldn't.

What would I do? It was a thought which had crossed my mind a million times and honestly, I didn't know. I just didn't know what I would do.

I promised myself that I would think about the future, to my family. There was nothing I could do for those struck by the event. I was one person in a group of five. My efforts to feed a small crowd at the airport showed how futile it was.

A hard and painful lesson I learned.

Moving forward meant getting what I needed from Tinker Airforce base and heading East.

Not far from where we were was the beginning of the darkness. A void I would soon enter.

The drive was long.

I swear I stared at my feet the entire time we drove. I couldn't look out the window, I really couldn't. I didn't want to see.

There was very little conversation in the van. It took two hours to get somewhere that should have taken less than a half hour under normal circumstances. But it wasn't normal. It wouldn't be normal as we knew it, for a long time.

We slowed down and then finally stopped. Wren announced, "We're here."

I knew by his quiet voice, almost silence, it wasn't good.

"Should we get out?" Trace asked.

"No. Stay here." Wren slowly opened his door.

I lifted my head, peering out the windshield.

The gate arm was down and Wren walked toward the booth. I didn't see any movement at all. There was a welcoming sign as if we arrived in Disneyland.

I watched Wren. He went into the booth and a minute later, the arm raised and he headed back to us, getting in the van.

He shut the door and breathed out before putting the van in gear. He handed me what looked like a pamphlet. "That's a map. Find something called the exchange."

I opened up the pamphlet and turned it over. "It's here." I pointed at the map.

"That's where we need to go," Wren said. "Look. There are thousands of people on this base. We need to be quiet. Get what we can and get out."

"I need a car to get home," I said. "Can we get one here?"

"We probably can. But our best bet is to get in and get out," Wren slowly drove forward. "Like I said, thousands of people lived here. So where are they?"

I didn't see a soul. I saw no one as we drove through the base. I focused on the map and navigating where to turn, but I kept looking out.

Where were these people? Had they vanished or were they all together somewhere waiting for a noise they could follow.

We passed a gas station that looked like something I would see in a main intersection of Cleveland. It was hard to believe we were on a military base.

There were cars at the station, two I noticed, parked at the pumps.

No people.

I made a mental note.

We turned the corner and the Exchange was there. It reminded me of a Target or Walmart. It was a big building with designated curbside parking.

We pulled in front and got out of the van. I looked around, still I saw no one.

Where was everyone? I had to remind myself it was a Sunday when it happened, maybe most people had a late start.

The automatic doors opened as soon as we stepped near them. It was eerie. Music played softly over the speaker system.

And it was the first time I saw a body since being on base.

A male worker, wearing his blue smock sat on the floor, his back against the cart station railing, head slumped to the side, eyes closed.

None of us spoke.

I wasn't sure why Trace did it, perhaps the doctor in him, but he crouched down a little with an extended hand for his neck.

Checking for a pulse.

His hand trembled a little as he moved in slowly. At first, I thought it was nervousness, but I knew better.

The moment his fingers touched the worker's neck …

Wham!

The worker lunged at Trace full force. He snapped out of that state and was up, arms extended, full body weight he blasted into Trace knocking him to the floor.

He raised one fist, pummeling down then as he raised the other, Will shot from the side, spearing him like a football player off his father, and entangled in a roll.

It wasn't like wrestlers, hitting from the low-down position, the worker raised up to strike and when he did … Bang.

A single shot.

His head cocked back and the force of the hit from the bullet set him back.

It happened so fast.

My eyes went from Trace, to Will, to the worker. Then finally, I raised my eyes to see Emily holding a gun.

Before anything happened, I knew, we all knew, that gunshot was a bell ringing out to anyone affected that could hear.

The locos.

A look of panic hit Wren's face and he ran to the front of the store. "The doors," he hollered as he ran.

I didn't know what to do. Trace was on the ground, trying to get up. Will had just stood, and Haley shifted left to right.

"What's happening?" she asked. "Oh my God, they're coming."

"Will!" Wren shouted. "Help me with this gate!"

Will took off toward Wren.

But the front door wasn't what Haley meant.

What she heard was in the store.

"Five or six. There are more of them than us," she said.

"How can you tell?" I asked.

"I'm counting."

Then I heard the running. It didn't sound like a stampede, but they cried out and those agonizing screams they made carried through the store and no doubt drew them from outside.

Here we were by the cart station in the opening of the store by some cracker display. Standing targets, we could get out of their way, they didn't see us.

Pulling Haley close, I rushed to Trace. "Hide her in the clothing rack." I told him, pointing to my right to the woman's section right after the customer service. "Go."

It took a second for me to realize his mouth was bloody, he nodded, took Haley's hand and turned. No sooner did he run toward the women's clothing, a man in uniform and female wearing store smock raged toward them.

Bang. Bang.

Two shots.

Two head shots.

Down they went.

I pivoted my body to see Emily holding the pistol, cupped with both hands in a stance as if she were in a shooting range. Calm, collective. Pivoting her body left and right, waiting and ready for anything to come at her.

A loco would emerge and she shot.

She didn't miss.

"Shelb, in my bag, I need another magazine. Hurry."

I hadn't a clue what she meant.

"It's black, rectangular it's in what looks like a green lunch box. Grab one. There are two more in there loaded."

She shot again, I flinched.

Shaking, I saw her bag on the ground and opened it. Immediately I saw the green lunch box. I opened it. Inside was another pistol and two of those rectangular things. I grabbed one. "Got it," I said.

"Put it in my back pocket."

I stood and did as she asked, placing it in her back pocket, again, jumping when she shot.

She didn't stop looking forward. Behind her was the door.

The locos ran at us, one, then two.

I was amazed and couldn't comprehend how she was doing it. She was like the first person shooter in a video game, firing at what came her way before it got close.

I waited for us to achieve some sort of next level, where things got harder, locos coming one after another.

But they didn't.

She ejected the magazine from the pistol, reached into her back pocket and loaded another inside.

We waited.

"Doors secure," said Will. "They're out there."

"Drawn to the shooting," added Wren. "I think once it stops, they'll go."

"I don't think they're any more in here," I said. "They would have come, right?"

Wren shrugged. "You know as much as I do."

"Will," I told him. "Your father is hiding Haley, tell them it's safe." I turned to Wren. "Should we call them out. Make noise."

Wren nodded. "Hello!" he shouted. "Anyone in here! Hello!"

I watched Emily, she was ready.

"I don't hear any more," whispered Haley. "Not in here."

Emily lowered her head at the same time she lowered her weapon. She placed it behind her back in the waist of her pants, then bent down and lifted the empty magazine.

"Thank you," I said to her. "I mean it, thank you."

"I was afraid to tell you guys I was carrying." She faced me. "I didn't want you scared."

"How did you learn to do that?" I asked.

"My father. I've been shooting since I was a kid. Hunting, too." She shifted suddenly, as if she heard something, reaching again for her weapon.

Watching her I realized that I had Emily all wrong.

She wasn't some weak soul that killed her family because she couldn't handle it, she was strong and did what she did to her family because she could.

It still didn't stop me from feeling guilty when I saw the bodies of those she shot down. The people were helpless victims of the event. I knew Emily didn't have a choice, she did it to save us.

I could see it on her face when she looked down at a body, she felt sad, maybe even conflicted.

They were feelings we'd all have to face.

Caught between looking at the locos as sick or as a threat to us.

Our day had barely started and already we were at a standstill.

We were safe in the store. They gathered by the thousands

outside, filling the parking lot, crammed like sardines.

They weren't trying to get in, which was a good thing. We'd be in trouble if they were.

For the time being, we had to make the best of it until we could figure out what to do.

CHAPTER TWENTY-NINE – MAKING THE BEST

Wren and Wil moved the bodies behind the customer service desk, out of sight. But the blood was still there.

Even though I had my purse backpack, I needed something bigger, especially if I was going to be on the road. I also needed a change of clothing and other items.

I grabbed a bigger backpack from another part of the store and headed to the women's section. Emily headed to the sporting goods.

Eventually, we'd meet up in the middle by the food.

Once I got some of the items needed, I took a break and had a sink bath, washing my body from hair to toe. It felt good to change my socks and everything else.

I actually felt better when I emerged, pushing the cart, arms on the handle like some sort of walker support.

It was filling up fast.

Ripping the tags off a tee shirt, I noticed Wren stood by the door, staring out. Leaving my cart, I walked over to him.

"Hey, you're not worried they'll get in here, are you?" I asked.

"Nah, the gate is down. They can't see. They only hear. Eventually, they'll move on or fall asleep."

"They're just moving about. How are they even alive?"

Trace's voice startled me. "They won't be for long. Unless they're finding a way to eat or drink, they'll pass away within a few days. And no." He looked at me. "I'm not saying we stay in the store a few days." He looked back out.

"For dying people," Wren said. "They sure have a lot of energy."

"It's fear," Trace replied. "Fear and adrenaline. They have no idea what is going on. What they hear is probably only noise, and if whatever occurred caused any brain injury, they can't process it. I can't explain what I felt when the man attacked me. He wasn't some rage monster, it was like he was defending himself."

"Maybe they think we're aliens," I said.

Trace shrugged. "Maybe."

I heard the running footsteps first and my heart skipped a beat, thinking another one was in the store.

Then Will called out.

"Dad." Will stopped running.

"What's wrong?" Trace asked.

"The televisions. I turned them on and hooked up one of those digital antennas."

He wasn't even finished talking when the three of us ran from the door to see what was going on.

"Guys wait,' Will called out.

I stopped running and turned back.

"I have no idea what they're saying. I think it's Italian."

It didn't matter to me what country or language they spoke, I was excited. Haley's theory was correct. Something she said with so much innocence.

While ninety-nine percent of our country was literally in the dark, the other side of the world was alive.

❦ ❦ ❦

It was a woman newscaster. The reception wasn't great and I didn't understand a word she was saying, but I understood the visuals. A world map was on the upper left side of the screen, areas in red were clearly the ones affected by the event. All of North America to Greenland, most of Europe was in the red. It ended mid-way through Italy and then some of Spain.

A straight line north to south from Rome and everything east of Rome and East of Norway was spared.

There was also a darker red that I believed was our 'darkness'.

It gave me a visual.

It gave me hope.

Video images as she spoke showed military trucks loaded with people. Makeshift hospital tents.

Trace handed Will back the phone. "Naples said they just started picking it up, too. They have a Linquist and they'll call us when they know something. It's like a Sky news sort of thing, I guess."

"A parte tutti i conflitti, le nazioni non colpite stanno mettendo in atto tentativi di salvataggio su vasta scala," the female newscaster said.

"I don't speak Italian," Wren said. "I'm fluent in Spanish. She's talking about conflicts being set aside. About a large-scale rescue attempt."

"In questo momento, sono in corso in Europa."

"In Europe." Wren said.

"I leader mondiali si stanno incontrando ora per discutere di uno sforzo globale e di come questo possa essere realizzato."

The visual accompanying her words showed several leaders, including the Russian president walking into a building.

"Leaders are coming together," Wren translated. "Something about planning a global effort."

Haley spoke up. "What about us? Are they going to rescue us?"

I placed my hand on her back. "I don't know. But it sounds like it."

"How?" Will tossed out his hands. "How do they rescue hundreds of millions of people. They'll be dead before they do. Sorry, Haley."

"We're not their problem," said Trace. "We're not." His eyes went back to the television. "Why is she showing the Vatican?"

Wren sighed out. "Because she said they don't know the cause, but it can only be an act of God."

"Great." Trace grumbled.

"I get that though," said Wren. "I do. Being the son of a preacher. I get it. Do I think it? No. But we can't rule it out."

"Yeah, yeah, we can," Trace said.

"We can't rule anything out," I added. 'Emily, what do you think?"

"You mean is it God?'

"I think it's God," snapped Will. "Seriously, the sun, it's all God. Right. How can anyone rescue us from God?"

"Dude," Wren said. "It's like a thousand years once the end starts."

"No."

"Yeah."

"No way. Dad?" Will asked.

"What the hell are you asking me for?" Trace barked.

"Does it matter?" Emily asked. "To me it doesn't. One way or another I am going to meet my maker soon enough and have to answer for what I did during this all."

"I think they'll get here eventually," Trace said. "It's a matter of when. But it won't be a rescue, it'll be a cleanup effort. So, we need to face the fact that those of us who survived. We're on our own."

At first, I thought the news broadcast was a glimmer of hope, but that hope only extended right now to the other side of the world.

And though I could see my family, my heart was already in the darkness, and before long I would enter it.

I was ready.

❊ ❊ ❊

It was another night away from my family, another night of

being stalled, but I knew it wouldn't be for long.

One more night.

The 'affected' outside became my entertainment once I grew tired of watching the same thing on the news.

I watched 'them'.

Our van was encircled, even if we were quiet, we couldn't get to it. I reminded everyone of the gas station and the cars parked at the pumps.

They had to have keys.

It was a block away. We could leave through the back door.

But by the time the affected calmed down enough for us to sneak out, it would be too late for me to drive east. It was better to stay, get what I needed and leave in the morning.

I watched them.

And it happened.

The humanity came through, I witnessed it and wanted to cry. In fact, I did.

They slowed down as the evening came, and exhausted by their constant movement, they lowered to the cold hard ground and rested.

Trace was right.

They were scared.

I watched them lay down to sleep and embrace whoever was closest to them.

Hold a stranger for comfort. They were seeking comfort.

I watched a woman near the door, extend her arms as she lay on the ground, bringing in the two people closest to her. I couldn't make out their expressions, but I could see how they held on to each other.

They were scared to death, internally they knew it was a matter of time, and in their darkness, they could do nothing.

I was so sorry. So sorry for them.

Too few of us could help the too many that were out there. In an instant I stopped looking at it as being silent to avoid attack, I looked at it as staying quiet enough so we didn't agitate them and they could find peace.

Peace in their final moments of fear and despair.

Leave them alone.

My heart broke.

After I watched them long enough, I made sure I had everything ready to go the next day.

Emily and I both had stuffed backpacks.

We could find more if we needed it, but it was enough to get us on our way.

I made my way to the Grinders Coffee shop near the front of the store, used the microwave to heat up a frozen Swedish meatball dinner, made a latte and sat at a table with a book I picked up.

It was quiet.

Haley and Emily went to sleep in the furniture department while Will and Wren set up a video game console in the entertainment department. The news still played, but I heard them more.

How Emily and Haley could sleep, I didn't know.

I was alone.

But not for long.

"High in sodium," Trace said as he said down at my table. "But I suppose that doesn't matter."

"I'm sorry."

"That meal. They're high in sodium."

"And this …" I lifted my latte. "Is high in caffeine. Now's not the time to worry about healthy living choices."

"No, it's not." He lifted his mug, one he probably picked up in housewares.

"Did you find the adult beverages?"

"I did. Want one?"

"No, I'm good."

Silence.

"I'm not," Trace said. "And I owe you an apology."

"For what?" I asked.

"Yesterday, I was pretty bad and argumentative with you."

"There's no need to apologize, we butted heads. It happens." I took a bite of my food.

"I am not like that, I am easy going, until …"

I glanced up.

"I was sober and agitated and needing a drink," Trace said. "It was probably the longest time I went without a drink. Twelve hours. That ought to tell you something."

"It's not for me to judge."

"But it is for me to explain. What was it you said, now's not the time for healthy living choices." He lifted his mug.

"Do you need to talk?" I asked.

"No. Not about this." He sipped. "Who cares, right?"

"Your son," I said.

"Yeah, he does. And eventually, I'll make it right. But right now, I'm not ready to."

"I understand."

"Okay, enough talk about my problems. I apologized and I needed to do that, and … you're really going in there?"

"I am."

"Accepted." Trace nodded. "I know we found the radiation detectors in here. There's an NBC training center on the other side of base, let's get you and Emily protective suits and masks before you take off. Can we do that?"

"Yes. I would appreciate that."

"And a radio. The phones will eventually go down. They'll be back up again, but they'll be down. I don't want to lose contact. I want to know what's going on. I can come with you, if you want."

"I would love all of you to come. But Wren needs to get to where he can help people, and Haley needs you and Will."

"That's why I don't want to lose contact," Trace said. "It's a big world. An empty world, and in a few weeks a lot emptier. Can you promise to let me know where you are?"

"I promise to do everything in my power to let you know where I am and how I am."

"Good." Trace reached across the table and placed his hand on mine. "We became friends at the end of the world. I'd like to keep that."

"Me, too."

"And …" He patted my hand. "That sodium induced meal smells and looks awfully good. Think I'll go grab one." He stood up.

"Freezer section, Ailse J. You might wanna grab two, they aren't very big."

"I'll be right back."

"Can you grab me another?"

Trace smiled. "I'll grab desert as well."

I shoved a meatball into my mouth, looking at the remaining few noodles in the black dish. I was still hungry. My appetite was back.

I flipped a page in the book, getting in a few more pages before Trace returned. In that little café I managed to not think about those outside and focus on the positive instead.

I felt better because I knew I wasn't leaving our small group on bad terms like some selfish rebel without a cause. We weren't parting forever, just parting until we could meet again.

I felt better because I knew in my heart and in my soul, this was the last delay.

No more.

When the next day came … I was going to head home.

CHAPTER THIRTY – LAST STOP

Morning came and we were all rested up. They were still out there in front of the building but scattered some and not moving as spry as they had the day before.

With our things gathered, we quietly made it out the back door.

The van was a lost cause. Anything we left in there we had to forget about. I had all I needed. Will had left his carry-on backpack in there.

We made it away from the exchange store and to the road without catching the attention of the locos.

They gathered in the parking lot, and seeing the amount of them took my breath away. I kept thinking how they clung to life, but life for them was fleeting.

We made it to the gas station. It was lit up and bright, no sign of people.

Three vehicles were at the pumps, doors open.

One of the cars had the gas hose still attached, but it had automatically stopped.

The keys were still in the ignition.

Another vehicle was an SUV. The keys were in there as well, but it had yet to be filled up.

It was time to go our separate ways.

I hadn't known Trace, Will, Wren or Haley for very long, but it was killing me to say goodbye.

We had been through the event together, it seemed only

right that we stayed together, yet we were parting.

I always thought groups who gathered in events like this stayed together, traveled to survive, like one big, sad road movie.

At that gas station, we said our goodbyes.

It felt as if I were saying goodbye to people I had known all my life.

We kept it brief, nothing long, nothing drawn out.

I was frightened that I was making a mistake, venturing into the darkness foolheartedly.

Leaving them felt like I was making a grave error. But I had the radio. The phone was possible as long as it would last.

I would try my hardest to stay in touch.

If that was possible.

With a map between the two front seats so we could navigate the back roads, we pulled away. I glanced up to the rearview mirror, watching them as we drove off.

As soon as we pulled through the gate of the base, I felt nervous. My insides trembled as we drove east. Not far from us was the darkness, at least it didn't look far, it loomed ominously, foretelling of trouble or something bad.

For a brief moment, staring at it, I thought about hitting the brakes, stopping and turning around.

I didn't.

I kept on driving.

※ ※ ※

The darkness created an optical illusion. It was a parallax. It was so massive I kept thinking we were closer than we were. But when we truly were upon it, it was evident.

We drove five hours until we stopped. Because I took the smaller car, not once did we have to use the gas cans.

The last we heard from Trace they had made it safely to the airport, were on board, and Wren was refueling. They were headed to Colorado.

We sent him several texts after that, but didn't hear anything back. The flight would be three hours give or take, so I wasn't going to relax until I knew they had landed.

We stopped shortly after the town of Salina on a two lane, secondary road with empty fields on each side and cornfields ahead.

There was something awe inspiring about the view of the darkness. Wicked, yet beautiful. The sun cut across the cornfields and a distinct line separated the light from the dark.

It didn't look as black being closer. It was one huge darkness, and it cast a shadow.

"Reading?" I asked Emily.

She pulled out the meter. It clicked slowly. "Normal."

"Let's drive a little closer and keep it on," I said.

"Agreed." She rubbed her eyes.

"Are you alright?"

"Headache, but I'm used to them. I grabbed stuff from the pharmacy at the exchange."

"Did Trace help you?"

Emily nodded.

I put the car in gear and drove slowly down the road. The meter still clicked slowly and steadily.

We made it maybe a half mile, just before the start of the cornfield, when Emily stated, "Stop."

"What's wrong." I stopped the car.

"Back up a little."

As soon as I looked backwards to go in reverse, I saw what she meant. A gravel driveway that led to a tiny, one-story yellow farmhouse. It sat at the end of the driveway, surrounded by a yard, a small shed nearby.

"If we need a place," Emily said. "That's the place."

"Why would we stop here?" I asked.

"Because we don't know how far into the dark we can go. You heard Trace. If it's too high, we have to wait. We run out of gas, you'll be sick in a day or two and dead if it's too high. You'll be no use to your family, dead or sick."

"Did he tell you what was too high?"

"He didn't give me a number, but he said this would tell us. Right now, it's green and saying no radiation levels detected."

"Maybe Napes is wrong. Maybe there isn't radiation in there."

"One way to find out."

I pulled forward.

Seven tenths of a mile, that was all we went and we stopped again. This time because I knew we were there.

Emily did a reading and it was normal. But just beyond the front end of the car was the shadow of the dark. It extended about twenty feet until it was darker, like looking into a room without windows or light.

The second, the very second, we crossed into the shadow the meter clicked faster.

"High normal," Emily said.

"Let's keep going."

"How about you stay here and let me," she said.

"Why would I do that?"

"Because it doesn't matter if I get dosed up, not to me. Can you let me do this?"

"We have the masks—"

"Shelb," she cut me off. "If it's too high those suits won't mean anything."

With a shivering breath, I nodded. "Okay. Go on."

Holding out the Geiger counter, Emily walked forward. A shadow cast upon her and then she sunk into the dark.

I could barely see her, I worried. What if there were some monsters on the other side of that dark?

She was a dark movement and not ten seconds after being swallowed by the darkness the meter sounded off.

First a clicking so fast it was a hum, and then it went high pitched and squealing.

The sound grew softer, not because it was less dangerous, but because she was walking.

"Emily!" I shouted. "Are you okay?"

"Yes," she replied. "Levels are dangerously high."

"Come out."

"Let me walk a little more!"

"Can you see anything?" I shouted.

"Barely. I have my flashlight."

I hated that I wasn't as brave as she was to walk in there. The sound faded farther and farther and then it grew louder. She was coming back.

She emerged out of the darkness.

"Are you okay?" I asked again.

"I am. I think for your sake we hold off. Just until the levels drop some. Just some."

Defeated, I lowered my head. "My family."

"I know. I know. But again, Shelb, you can't be any good to them if you get sick."

"They're in there," I said. "In that radiation."

"If it goes all the way to Cleveland. We don't know. Trace and Wren both said radiation drops every day. Let's go back to that farmhouse and wait. I'll check again tomorrow."

I nodded my agreement. "How high was it?"

She didn't answer.

"How high is the radiation?" I asked again.

Emily pursed her lips, looked down and then after a moment looked back up. "To high to be measured."

CHAPTER THIRTY-ONE – STOPPING

There was one body in the farmhouse.

An older man, his age hard to tell. He was on the kitchen floor between the small four chairs, brown table and the sink. A cup of coffee was on the table and some half-eaten toast. The position of his body told me he fell out of the chair.

Together Emily and I carried him out. I hid any pain I felt because of the way Emily was being. She was trying to be strong, and if I said I was in pain, I knew she would just do it alone.

We took him out to the yard and immediately, Emily started digging a grave.

"If we're going to use his home, this is the least we can do," she said.

I offered to help and she declined. Emily stated she'd let me know when the grave was done and then I could help her.

In the meantime, I checked out the house.

A kitchen, living room, bathroom and two small bedrooms. The man's life was in that house.

We needed to respect that.

The power was still on, he had milk in the fridge along with vegetables.

A yellow old-fashioned push-button phone was on the wall of the kitchen that looked like it was something from the 80's. Sunflower wallpaper, metal cupboards.

I had Naples' number and I lifted the phone and called.

It rang, but there was no answer.

I worried.

I hadn't heard from Trace and now Naples wasn't answering. I sent a text to Trace and to Will letting them know where we were.

In the meantime, I explored the small home. We would be in the farmhouse for at least a few days. It was homey and clean, a home-made knitted blanket hung over a reclining chair in the living room.

The man's shoes were by the front door, neatly placed on the mat.

The bed in the bigger bedroom was made, and the smaller bedroom, while it had a bed, was mainly used for storage.

The pictures on the table by the living room front window told me a lot about his life.

The pictures spanned a long life, a wife, children, possibly grandchildren.

I guessed his wife had passed because the pictures of her stopped when she was still young.

Stalled again.

It seemed every effort I made to get home, to find my family, was blocked by another obstacle.

This time something invisible.

Radiation.

A part of me wanted to say the hell with it and just barrel through, but I thought about what Emily had said.

What good would I be blasting through the radiation and getting sick if my family needed me?

Then again, if my family was in there with that radiation, then what was the point?

A good part of me resolved I would never see them again. What happened to them was beyond my control.

I could stop.

If I did, then the rest of my life would be spent wondering. What if I went in there? What if I had found them?

No, I knew when the time came, I had to venture through.

Even if it was just to confirm and find out.

I watched Emily through the window of the kitchen, she took frequent breaks. There was a bottle of water in the fridge and as I left to take it to her, my phone rang.

I answered it. It was Will. "Oh, tell me you're okay."

"We're fine. We just landed and wanted to check it. Haley's fine."

"Thank you. We had to stop. We made good distance. But radiation was too high."

"Give it a few days?" he asked.

"That's the plan."

"Where are you now?"

"Little bit outside of Salina Kansas. At a cute farmhouse on something called Magnolia Road. We'll stay here, it's close enough to check the radiation levels."

"Listen," will said. "Once we get into base, I'll try to find someone with knowledge to give you guys good advice about the radiation."

"That would be great. In case the cells go down, there's a landline here. I'll call you from that so you have the number. Right now, tell everyone I'm going to help Emily bury the guy that lived in this house."

"Are you well enough to do that?" Will asked.

I glanced out the window at Emily. "I think I am. She needs help."

I said my goodbye to Will, confident I would talk to him again, and before I went out with Emily, I made sure he had the landline number.

Holding some water, I made my way to Emily. Her hands rested on the shovel and she breathed heavily.

"Here," I handed her the water. "Take a break."

"I'm just about done."

I looked down at the hole, it wasn't six feet, but it was deep enough to cover him with the dirt. "You're done."

Emily drank her water and exhaled. "I never buried my family, I just left. What is wrong with me?"

"You were distraught, grieving, in shock. All of those things."

She whimpered a small sob and stifled it with a sip of water. "There's no excuse for anything that I done. Buring this man, going with you, I need to atone. Nothing will make up for what I did, but I need to. Not because I'm dying, but because, you know?"

I nodded and looked over my shoulder to the horizon. I didn't know what to say to her, no words would comfort or make her feel better. I could only help her bury this man. One of the many things she had on her bucket list of good deeds.

She teetered on the edge of emotional darkness as we literally were at the edge of the end of world, facing it, an unknown.

As we waited to go in there, it didn't matter what we did in our lives before this moment, I just knew, after we stepped through, we would get answers. Answers Trace was chasing.

We'd get them because we were going in there and nothing from the moment, we stepped in would ever be the same again.

CHAPTER THIRTY-TWO – A FRIEND

Six days.
Every day for six days, Emily walked into the darkness and did a reading.
It was having an effect on her and I could see it.
Her skin was paler, she was more tired.
But the readings barely decreased as we were told they would.
Some so-called expert in Colorado told us a good level, that we could tolerate several hours if not more. But it didn't reach that.
I grew antsy and sad each day that passed, knowing that it was another day I couldn't help my family if they were alive.
On day seven, a single visitor in a military Humvee arrived.
Colonel Mallory Higgins.
She was alone with no soldiers, and she showed up in her vehicle with a gas can strapped on the roof.
She had driven from Nevada, alone. Her stops along the way were military bases and towns she knew were operational, and her mission was to find and join us.
Malory had gotten our location from Wren and wanted to go into the dark.
She had nothing to lose.
I was sitting on the front porch of the house, Emily was taking a nap, when Mallory pulled up.
She stepped from the vehicle and looked around. "Wow, this

is amazing."

I worried at first that the military would come because they feared we weren't capable enough to go in there.

Quite the opposite.

Mallory came because she wanted to be a part of it.

"So, you remember me?" she asked when she stepped from the vehicle.

"Seeing that it hasn't been that long ago," I replied. "Yes, I do. Can I help you? I mean, why are you here?"

"I came to go in."

"We're fine. We don't need help."

"That's kind of insulting. And flattering," Mallory said. "I'm alone. Not sure how much helping power I have other than a decent vehicle, some bio suits and weapons. But I'm not here to help because you need it, I'm here to be a part of it. When word reached me that you were going in, I wanted to be there. I need to be in there. I want to know what's in there. That's the center of what has happened, I truly believe it."

"I do, too."

"My husband is affected, blind, not deaf, but easily agitated and confused. We had to confine him. My three daughters are dead and their kids are gone, my grandkids disappeared. What does that?"

I shook my head. "You said yourself people are saying it's God."

"I grew up my entire life being good and believing, I have a hard time believing God would do something like this. No, this was nature. That's why I'm here if you'll have me."

"Absolutely." I stood. "Come in. Relax, I just pumped water and it's in the fridge."

"There's a well?"

"Yep. Come on in." I opened the screen porch door for her.

She grabbed a large duffle bag and backpack from her car and stepped up to the porch, giving me a look of thank you as she did.

When she passed through the threshold, I realized she wasn't coming as military, even though she was in uniform. I realized she came as a mother, wife, grandmother, looking for answers.

Much like me.

After I thought about it, I liked that Mallory was joining us.

Together we weren't military or fighters. We were three women, mothers, all going in together. I couldn't think of a more unstoppable force.

CHAPTER THIRTY-THREE – GOING IN

Callum.

An odd name for a man in his fifties, but Callum Harrison was the name of the man who lived in the house we now occupied.

He was the man we buried in the yard.

For over a week I spent time getting to know him and his family. The children in the pictures were not his own, they were nieces and nephews.

All the pictures in the house but there were never any family photos. Just Callum and his wife Anita.

Later in his life there were lots of children in photos around him.

The cards and notes to Uncle Cal told me a lot.

A simple man with a simple life.

A man who died while enjoying his breakfast.

I didn't have any notions of returning to Callum's home after we ventured into the darkness, but I left it as an option.

When we packed up to go, a part of me didn't feel as if I were saying goodbye to the ranch.

I felt as if we'd return eventually.

I loved it there.

Maybe when I found my family, I would bring them back here.

But it was time to go.

Three women, three personalities.

We took the military truck or whatever it was.

It had the lighting system we needed and was much better than the compact car we had taken from that gas station in Oklahoma City.

Mallory had a different route mapped out. She worked it out herself before coming to us. In the evening before day ten, she explained the route while we sipped on broth and defrosted bread from the freezer.

Traveling Magnolia Road would take us through farmland for a long time. If we wanted to see a city, we needed to take her route. Even though she said she would do whatever we decided.

We opted for her route.

Kansas City, as scary as the prospect seemed, was two hours away.

It was a day in a second.

Just before entering the dark, it was as bright as noon on a summer's day, within seconds of driving it seemed as if it were twilight time.

Then it was dark.

Dark was an understatement.

The military Humvee style truck was equipped with lights. Headlights, flood lights, fog lights and spots.

All of which Mallory turned on as we drove down the secondary highway. It seemed like something out of a horror movie. The road wasn't jammed packed with vehicles, but through the beams of the lights, we would see a car abandoned or crashed. Pushing into a guard rail or another car. The view of the vehicles would creep up into the light out of the blackness and we'd weave around it.

I wondered if our eyes would adjust. If eventually, we would be able to see a little bit. But on that road, we only passed vehicles.

I didn't see any bodies or people.

An hour into the drive, halfway to Kansas City, we stopped. Not because we couldn't go forward, but because Mallory wanted to check to see if she could get a signal on the phone or radio.

She stepped out and when she did, I couldn't see her. It was crazy.

I kept my hand on the handle of the passenger door.

"Reading?" I asked Emily.

"Elevated normal, borderline yellow."

"What does that mean?"

"It's a high normal, but if radiation gets any higher, the color will go from green to yellow indicating danger."

The only reason I could see Emily in the car was the glow from the meter. Otherwise, she would have been swallowed as well.

It had been several minutes and I opened the door.

"What are you doing?" Emily asked.

"I want to see if she's okay and I want to see what it's like out there."

"What if something is out there? What if something got her?"

"Nothing is out there." I glanced at the windshield. "Nothing. I'll be back."

I opened the door, the cab light came on and I stepped out and down to the road.

The moment I shut the door, the light faded, but looking back I could see the glow of the meter. When turned, back facing the truck, it was just dark. I lifted my hand and couldn't see it.

I found it ironic that even though I had my sight, out there on the road I was like millions of others. I couldn't see.

"Mallory!" I called for her, not loud, but it didn't need to be loud.

"Here. On the phone. Letting them know what we see," she replied.

Thinking, 'did you tell them we see nothing', I felt my way around the truck. The side, the hood, making my way to the sound of her voice.

I was close and then I saw the glow of her phone. Light barely penetrated the darkness. Her cheek, and part of her hand were like a vignette against a black backdrop.

"I'll keep you posted," she said. "Right now, we're still seventy miles from the city. Yes, sir. Thank you, sir."

The beep of the phone told me she was done and for a brief second it was black again, until she used the phone flashlight.

"Ready?" she asked,

"Yes." I felt my way to the driver's door. "What was the point?"

"The point?" she asked.

"Of stopping and calling."

"I got everything we needed, equipment, weapons, suits, on the contingency that we check in."

"Fair enough." I heard the door to the truck open and the interior light was my guide. I climbed inside, sliding over to the passenger seat and looked back at Emily. "Are you alright?"

"Yeah, I'm fine."

I nodded and smiled, but I knew she wasn't. Each day her color grew worse, she was pale, and her eyes dark. I didn't know if it was her medical condition or the fact that she kept going into the highly radiated areas.

We were all back in the truck. Mallory drove forward.

It wouldn't be long before we reached Kansas City.

A major city in the dark. That one city would tell us everything.

❋ ❋ ❋

The small flashlight fit in the palm of my hand and following Mallory's instructions, I opened the glove box and pulled out the map.

A map of Kansas City.

She slowed down, then stopped, leaning over and looking at the map. "There," she said. "This is where we'll get off the exit."

"What are we looking for?" I asked.

"Anything."

Emily spoke from the back seat. "That's pretty open. So, we're not looking for anything in particular."

"No," Mallory replied. "This is a huge city. What we see here should be indictive of what happened everywhere. This is still what can be considered the edge of the darkness. Anything farther east has to be worse."

I didn't want to hear that. I wanted to find that Kansas City was fine. That we'd see lights speckling in the darkness. Glimmers of hope of survivors.

Imagine our view.

Darkness surrounded a beam of light.

Blackness, blackness, then a car.

Blackness, blackness, a truck.

Appearing in the light we shone, not for long, just until we passed. The exit sign was the same way.

We drove, watching that right side white line and then we saw the exit sign.

Kansas City was huge.

There were no shapes of skyscrapers, nothing.

Nothing.

Dark.

Black.

Pulling off the exit, we entered the city. We had no issues, until we turned down a street. Cars and trucks blocked the roads. It was wreckage, and it was apparent that whatever happened was instantaneous, causing the vehicles to immediately crash.

Emily leaned forward. "What exactly are we looking for here?" she asked.

"Anything," Mallory answered. "My goal is to get through the city and see."

She stopped the truck and controlled the spotlights, shining them upward and across the structures in front of us.

They were untouched, undamaged, and dark. No flicker of lights like I hoped. No signs of life, but we were only on the outskirts of the city.

Maybe just maybe when we got into the thick of downtown, we'd find someone.

We followed the map.

"We won't find anything here,' said Mallory. "This was an industrial section of town. Once we cross the river, we may see more. Well, as well, as we could see."

"The river," I muttered.

"What about it?" Mallory asked. "Just a thought. Those poor people trying to walk, to find their way home, falling off or into things."

"Most aren't going anywhere, from what I've seen," said Mallory. "Would you?"

"Survival is possible without sight and sound," Emily said. "But they aren't thinking when it happens. They're in shock."

"Cryng out for help," I added. 'But unable to hear their own voices. It's easy for me to say, well, I would get a stick and feel my way around. And I am sure some did, but the majority. I saw the woman on the airplane, the confusion and fear and panic. There are not enough people to help."

"We can try," said Mallory. "All do our part. We have to."

"Hey, guys," Emily said softly. "What is that? On the right. I think I see a light but are my eyes playing tricks on me."

If her eyes were playing tricks, mine were too. I saw it. In the midst of the black, I saw a light. But it wasn't like a candle flickering in a window. It was more of a glow like a phone or the meter did.

Mallory slowed down. "Let me see the map. We need to follow that."

"Is it safe?" I asked.

"We'll find out."

CHAPTER THIRTY-FOUR – WHERE THERE'S A GLOW, THERE'S HOPE

A multitude of things raced through my mind as we drove in the dark toward that light. It seemed to come from between buildings and was hard to say what it was.

The paranoid person in me feared some sort of space alien ship.

We'd soon find out.

We had to backtrack some, going south in order to get to a bridge across the river.

That was scary.

Hearing the sound under the wheels, the hollow sound, which told me we were on a bridge. The darting view of a car here and there in the headlight. But the glow, the light was now ahead of us.

Looking at the map, the only thing ahead of us was marked on the map as the Kansas Downtown Airport. I didn't know what that was, it didn't seem big enough on the map to be a major airport, but it was in the middle of the city.

The light didn't seem to get bigger the closer we drew, it seemed bright. Not bright enough to cut through the dense darkness.

At the end of the bridge, Mallory turned right, there were two collided cars, and then I saw a dancing light.

At least it looked like dancing lights, cutting through the dark, small specks.

They didn't move like flashlights, more steadily.

"Oh my God," I said. "It is aliens."

"What?" Mallory laughed. "What are you talking about?"

"The big glow is a mother ship and those are drones."

"No. I don't think they are. They're too low," Mallory replied. "I think they're ..."

Before Malory could finish, the identity of the dancing lights was uncovered.

They grew closer, bigger, brighter.

Headlights.

Six sets of them headed our way.

"What the hell?" Mallory asked.

Emily leaned toward us. "Those look like big lights."

"They are." Mallory stopped when the vehicles pulled up, forming a blockade around us.

I couldn't see what the vehicles were, just the strong headlights and spotlights they put on us.

It brightened the entire cab of Mallory's vehicle.

Then came the flashlights and out of the truck walked two figures.

Shadowed, and they had weapons.

Once they stepped before the headlights, I could see the two people were men and they looked military.

It was still hard to tell.

"Reading," Mallory asked Emily.

"We're in the yellow. Still low though."

The two men shouldered their weapons and approached the driver's side.

They were illuminated to us by the spotlights.

"They're soldiers," Mallory said as they came close. "But they're not ours."

"What do you mean?" I asked.

"They're not US soldiers," she said.

"Who are they?"

"I don't know," she replied. "But we're about to find out."

※ ※ ※

The one thing I had forgotten about, it was a big deal at the time, but it slipped my mind in the time that passed since the event.

I was so focused on getting home.

The United States of America still had a president, and he found out that there were mass rescue efforts on the other side of the world, he did what he could to reach out.

Mallory wasn't wrong.

The soldiers were ROK. The South Korean Army, neither of the two soldiers spoke fluent English, but enough to convey for us to follow them.

What choice did we have? We followed their vehicles to the downtown airport where they had a base set up.

Giant spotlights lit the area, there were tents and trucks, and a couple armored vehicles.

According to Mallory it didn't look like a long-term set up.

I looked around in wonder at all the people, hundreds, maybe.

Why Kansas City?

She was still in uniform, and they seemed to respect that. We were brought into a bigger tent, that looked like a communications set up.

There an older man came in, distinguished, he introduced himself as Colonel Park.

He took a double look at Emily, and I thought that was odd at first, until I saw how pale she looked.

"Are you all right?" I whispered to her.

"Just tired and my head," she replied.

"We have a medical team," Colonel Park said. "If you wish to see them."

Emily shook her head.

"I am quite shocked, we all were when we spotted the light of your vehicle," said the colonel.

"We were shocked as well when we saw yours," I replied.

He smiled and sat at the table with us. "When we first saw you Colonel," he nodded to Mallory. "I checked, there is no American Military in this area yet, then I realized your companions were civilian. What brings you into the zone?"

"Can I ask that you answer that question first?" Mallory asked.

"Absolutely," he replied. "We are part of the Global Rescue Operations. We were assigned to the region for search and rescue. We arrived in the Gulf of Mexico last week and our area is Missouri and north. We are part of thousands that arrived to enter the zone in America. It's massive. A great deal of the black covers a great deal of your country."

"Have you found anyone?" asked Emily.

"Some, yes. Very sick. None here yet in this city," he replied. "The southern teams have reported finding more. Sadly, most are casualties. Anyone found alive, has lost their sight and ability to hear, they are suffering from radiation sickness as well."

Then I asked. "We have run into groups that are dangerous. They can't see, but they can hear. Have you?"

He shook his head. "Not here in America, not in the zone, but there have been reports in other places. The boom, as we call it, caused damage to the brain. In most it caused the loss of hearing, in some, it caused the loss of reason. There has been some success with medication. It calms them. We're still early in the process, there are plans in motion."

"Plans?" I asked.

"On how to help those who survived. We believe there are still a lot of people alive in the zone, they just can't find their way out. Now you," he said. "What brings you into the zone."

Mallory answered first, "Curiosity and answers."

"My family," I said. "I wasn't home when it happened. I wanted to be home by now, but we took readings at the edge and they were high."

Colonel Park nodded. "As they would be, this area is close to the impact site. Well, a thousand miles or so, but the radiation spread in a circular way, which is unusual."

Mallory shook her head slowly. "Impact site? Something hit us?"

"Not like a bomb, but flare or whatever it was, hit us, we still can't get close to the impact area to get soil samples. Eventually though. So, teams are searching a good distance from around it."

"I don't understand," I said. "It was a flare, I didn't think CMEs could physically blast earth."

"It's not like a meteor impact or bomb. I will demonstrate." Colonel Park stood and walked across the tent to a desk. He spoke to a woman there then returned to us. "This brilliant demonstration was shown to me, I did not come up with it." He placed a map of the US on the table. "We are here." He circled the area. "This is what happened. Let's say this match is the flare." He ignited it, let it burn a second or two, then blew it out. While red and smoldering, he dropped it on the map. Immediately, the map sizzled and the outer area around the match turned brown and black. "Actually, that burn mark is quite comparable to the actual size. When it hit, it sent a blast of light nearly three quarters around the globe. Followed by the sound, which was worse on those closer to the ground. We don't know why."

Mallory pointed. "The burned areas are completely destroyed."

"Done, obliterated like a nuclear flash. Everyone inside was incinerated, buildings demolished. There is zero chance of survival. It was so hot, it evaporated most of this lake."

He pointed down, I didn't look, I was afraid to look. Finally, I drew up the courage. "Do you know where in the US? Where is gone?"

After another nod, he went back to the desk and returned with a tablet. I watched him swipe his finger across it. "We have images. Drone images."

"Cleveland, just tell me," I said. "Was Cleveland in that area?"

"Is that where your family is?" Colonel Park asked.

"Yes."

"I am truly, very sorry." He handed me the tablet.

My heart screamed in pain. I felt it in my chest, it was about to explode. Every bit of my being and soul wanted to collapse.

I need to cry, sob, scream, get angry, all and every emotion.

I needed to grieve or die.

I needed to leave.

My journey was over, my quest was done.

Cleveland was right smack in the middle of the impact site. It was gone. My family was gone.

There was no need to go forward.

CHAPTER THIRTY-FIVE – USELESS

I was devastated and broken but not blindsided.

I knew.

Deep down in my gut I knew my family was gone despite my heart wanting so badly to believe they survived.

I saw the light, the flash. I witnessed their end and didn't even know it at the time. I was too busy fighting with my husband and being tossed about that bathroom to even conceive the thought they were gone.

But I knew.

What was wrong with me? I wanted to cry, I so badly needed to cry. But I couldn't, I hadn't shed a tear. My soul was crushed, but I couldn't cry, I would.

I was in shock, even though it was news I expected, a numbing shock took over me. After getting the confirmation, I stepped out of that tent and walked until I couldn't see anything,

Just blackness.

Void of life out there, like I felt. Completely, utterly alone in the world. A world that was on its way out.

My purpose was gone.

It had been over two weeks since the event. Two weeks since I saw my family. Was it all an adjustment time? All the bad I had seen and felt, was it a way to prepare me for what I would face?

It would be a lie to say I didn't think about their deaths when I had quiet moments, what I would do, how I would handle it.

There are no answers when uncertainty lingers.

Emily found me and was out of breath. "There you are."

I stood at the edge of camp not far from one of those large spotlights. She walked up to me.

"I'm sorry, I am so sorry, Shelb."

I grabbed her hand. "Thank you."

"We're worried, come back to the tent."

"I will."

"Please tell me you're not walking out there."

I shook my head. "I'm not. The only thing that makes it bearable is I know they felt nothing. It happened too fast. But it left me nothing. I have nothing left of them. No pictures, I can't go home."

"You have memories and your phone pictures."

"Until they both fade."

"Then you try not to let that happen," Emily said. "Colonel Park said we could stay. They move out in three days. They need help in the cities. He said he could get me to the medical ship."

"Is that what you want?"

"I don't know what I want," Emily said. "I know I want to do some good. What about you?"

"I want to die."

"Shelb—"

"But I won't. I am all that's left of my family. Even in this screwed up world, I need to stay alive so they can. As hard as it will be."

"No one wants a decision now. Take all the time in the world to think about it, to grieve."

"I will. But for now …" I squeezed her hand and then released it. "I'm going to stay out here a little bit longer."

"Okay." Emily backed up and stopped. "You're not going to—"

"No, I'm going to stay right here, I promise."

"I'll check back."

"Thank you."

I returned to staring out, my arms folded against my chest. My physical being had finally started to heal, somehow, I knew my inner being would take longer than a broken bone.

It was a strange feeling, one of loss and being lost, yet not wanting to be found or have guidance.

I didn't know what was happening to the world. A part of me felt it wasn't over, that everything we faced was a prelude to a destructive orchestration that was yet to come.

It was not the world I woke up to two weeks earlier, and it would never be again.

Only time would tell what would become of the world and of me. And time, as long as I was alive, was something I had plenty of.

CHAPTER THIRTY-SIX – NEXT WORLD ORDER

The human race is resilient. Against all odds, their inner instinct is to survive.

I stayed with Colonel Park's brigade for three days and then I left. Colonel Park had me driven back to the farmhouse.

I was alone in a truck with a man that didn't speak English.

It was a long quiet ride.

Mallory continued on with them, and so did Emily.

How did our little group get so fractured?

We were scattered across the country. Yet, when the world fell apart, we were together.

Callum Harrison was his name, the man that owned and lived in the farmhouse.

I decided that was where I would stay until I figured out what my part in everything would be.

Unlike Emily or Mallory, I didn't have the urge to help. I self-taught myself farming while watching the dark of the dead zone each and every morning on the horizon.

My days were spent making sure my phone stayed charged and I kept in contact with everyone. Staring at pictures of my family, watching videos.

The day the power went down in the farmhouse, I felt as if it were my end of the world. Or that I need power, I needed my phone. It was the only link I had to those I had lost.

I stayed in contact with everyone through the landline. A once-a-week call.

Trace was doctoring again. Will was teaching the children that had survived and Wren, well, he was flying.

Each of them always gave me updates on what they were doing.

My updates were simple, I was still there. Still hanging in there.

The days turned into weeks, then months. Mallory and a small group of soldiers came to see me four months after I left her, she brought a generator and news that Emily had passed away.

She had gone to sleep after a seizure and never woke up.

It saddened me, but I knew Emily was where she needed to be.

Mallory was impressed that I was keeping it going alone.

Alone is the way I wanted it to be, and I wasn't really some survival guru. The town of Salina had ample supplies that I retrieved often.

I pushed a shopping cart there and back the three miles.

I don't know if it was during that visit or the next one that Mallory asked me if I would be interested in being a survival station. A place where those who emerge from the dead zone could find food, comfort and help.

It was a ridiculous notion. No one was coming out of the dead zone. So, I agreed.

Once it was set in motion, they'd bring me what I needed.

And they did.

It was a good year maybe, I had lost track of time, when the monthly truck with supplies began to arrive. As if I would use them. They brought me a radio and gas for the generator.

I was officially a receiving station.

At first, I looked at it as some sort of joke, then I found myself, every single day, sitting out on that porch watching and waiting, hoping someone would come through.

Of course, I did my chores and trips to town, but I watched

the horizon.

I wondered how those affected by the event would find their way out.

Again, humans are resilient.

Those who managed to survive the harsh first few weeks of their sudden blindness and deafness, learned, adapted and lived.

The global initiative helped with a lot of that.

But still, many of them died of hunger, thirst, alone in the silent darkness. A horrendous way to die.

There were signs placed in the dead zone. They had a beacon that flashed a light for those who could see. A sound for those who could hear, and a pulse vibration that could be felt for those who could neither see nor hear. It would give them something to follow.

It worked south of me, several people came through.

Including locos.

I was ready for anything. But nothing happened.

No one came through.

With the exception of the trucks, I was alone. I preferred it that way.

Wren and Trace came to visit me a few times, each time asking me to come to Colorado.

I refused.

I was content. So, content that I started to believe that since I never saw that my family was dead, that maybe somehow they weren't. That maybe … somehow, they'd come down that dirt road out of the dead zone.

Watching the horizon, hopeful that my family, or someone would walk through, was my purpose.

That and waiting for the world to end.

It never recovered, never bounced back to where it was, not even close. Not after nearly two years.

No internet, no cell phones, no people.

Even though I could see, it was a silent world.

Perhaps a normal and bustling world would return.

I still wasn't convinced it was over. Something bigger was

going to happen.

I felt it in my bones every day as I watched the blackened sky of the dead zone. There was never an explanation why it remained dark.

It just did.

I wish my story, my journey had a happy ending. One where my family was with me at the farmhouse. Where Trace, Wren, Will and Emily were laughing over a BBQ, eating fresh corn I picked from the field.

That was a fantasy. One I played in my mind every so often when loneliness crept in.

To me, most of the time it was a world spiraling to an end and I had a front row seat right there on that front porch.

I had come to terms with my solo destiny. My job.

And though the world seemed to be rushing to a hopeless finish line, I wasn't. It may have seemed it, but I wasn't.

I sat there every day, watching, waiting, hoping.

Because one day someone would come through. I believed it.

Someone would walk from the darkness and seeing them would tell me, 'Hey, it's not over. It's not over yet.'

BOOKS BY THIS AUTHOR

300 Days

Forty years later, the pain of his personal tragedy still echoes within John Hopper. He retreats to the small town, Ripley, West Virginia, and is content being alone and in peace. He spends his evenings as an amateur podcast host, anonymously broadcasting rants about what is wrong with the world. Through a faithful listener and scientist, Jarvis, John finds out about the impending comet impact, possibly, an extinction level event.

With no beneficiary and ample time to prepare, John uses all his money to get everything he needs to survive the end of the world ... alone. What John doesn't realize is that meeting Yely, the problematic teenage girl who moved in next door, changes things.

All may not be as expected. John not only finds himself bringing people into his shelter, he learns that Ripley, the predicted safest place on earth, may very well become one of the worst places imaginable

Printed in Great Britain
by Amazon